Ernest William Hornung

My Lord Duke

Ernest William Hornung

My Lord Duke

ISBN/EAN: 9783337032289

Printed in Europe, USA, Canada, Australia, Japan

Cover: Foto ©Andreas Hilbeck / pixelio.de

More available books at **www.hansebooks.com**

MY LORD DUKE

BY

E. W. HORNUNG

NEW YORK
CHARLES SCRIBNER'S SONS
1897

Norwood Press

J. S. Cushing & Co. — Berwick & Smith

Norwood Mass. U.S.A.

CONTENTS

CONTENTS

MY LORD DUKE

MY LORD DUKE

CHAPTER I

THE HEAD OF THE FAMILY

The Home Secretary leant his golf-clubs against a chair. His was the longest face of all.

"I am only sorry it should have come now," said Claude apologetically.

"Just as we were starting for the links! Our first day, too!" muttered the Home Secretary.

"*I* think of Claude," remarked his wife. "I can never tell you, Claude, how much I feel for you! We shall miss you dreadfully, of course; but we couldn't expect to enjoy ourselves after this; and I think, in the circumstances, that you are quite right to go up to town at once."

"Why?" cried the Home Secretary warmly. "What good can he do in the Easter holidays? Everybody will be away; he'd much better come with me and fill his lungs with fresh air."

"I can never tell you how much I feel for you," repeated Lady Caroline to Claude Lafont.

"Nor I," said Olivia. "It's too horrible! I don't believe it. To think of their finding him after all! I don't believe they *have* found him. You've made some mistake, Claude. You've forgotten your code; the cable really means that they've *not* found him, and are giving up the search!"

Claude Lafont shook his head.

"There may be something in what Olivia says," remarked the Home Secretary. "The mistake may have been made at the other end. It would bear talking over on the links."

Claude shook his head again.

"We have no reason to suppose there has been a mistake at all, Mr. Sellwood. Cripps is not the kind of man to make mistakes; and I can swear to my code. The word means, 'Duke found — I sail with him at once.'"

"An Australian Duke!" exclaimed Olivia.

"A blackamoor, no doubt," said Lady Caroline with conviction.

"Your kinsman, in any case," said Claude Lafont, laughing; "and my cousin; and the head of the family from this day forth."

"It was madness!" cried Lady Caroline softly. "Simple madness — but then all you poets *are* mad! Excuse me, Claude, but you remind me of the Lafont blood in my own veins — you make it boil. I feel as if I never could forgive you! To turn up your nose at one of the oldest titles in the three kingdoms; to think twice about a purely hypothetical heir at the antipodes; and actually to send out your solicitor to hunt him up! If that was not Quixotic lunacy, I should like to know what is?"

The Right Honourable George Sellwood took a new golf-ball from his pocket, and bowed his white head mournfully as he stripped off the tissue paper.

"My dear Lady Caroline, *noblesse oblige* — and a man must do his obvious duty," he heard Claude saying, in his slightly pedantic fashion. "Besides, I should have cut a very sorry figure had I jumped at the throne, as it were, and sat there until I was turned out. One knew there *had* been an heir in Australia; the only thing was to find out if he was still alive; and Cripps has done so. I'm bound to say I had given him up. Cripps has written quite hopelessly of late. He must have found the scent and followed it up during the last six weeks; but in another six he will be here to tell us all about it — and we shall see the Duke. Meanwhile, pray don't waste your sympathies upon *me*. To be perfectly frank, this is in many ways a relief to me — I am only sorry it has come now. You know my tastes; but I have hitherto found it expedient to make a little secret of my opinions. Now, however, there can be no harm in my saying that they are not entirely in harmony with the hereditary principle. You hold up your hands, dear Lady Caroline, but I assure you that my seat in the Upper Chamber would have been a seat of conscientious thorns. In fact I have been in a difficulty, ever since my grandfather's death, which I am very thankful to have removed. On the other hand, I love my — may I say my art? And luckily I have enough to cultivate the muse on, at all events, the best of oatmeal; so I am not to be pitied. A good quatrain, Olivia, is more to me than coronets; and the society of my literary friends is dearer to my heart than that of all the peers in Christendom."

Claude was a poet; when he forgot this fact he was also an excellent fellow. His affectations ended with his talk. In appearance he was distinctly desirable. He had long, clean limbs, a handsome, shaven, mild-eyed face, and dark hair as short as another's. He would have made an admirable Duke.

Mr. Sellwood looked up a little sharply from his dazzling new golf-ball.

"Why go to town at all?" said he.

"Well, the truth is, I have been in a false position all these months," replied Claude, forgetting his poetry and becoming natural at once. "I want to get out of it without a day's unnecessary delay. This thing must be made public."

The statesman considered.

"I suppose it must," said he, judicially.

"Undoubtedly," said Lady Caroline, looking from Olivia to Claude. "The sooner the better."

"Not at all," said the Home Secretary. "It has kept nearly a year. Surely it can keep another week? Look here, my good fellow. I come down here expressly to play golf with you, and you want to bunker me in the very house! I take it for the week for nothing else, and you want to desert me the very first morning. You shan't do either, so that's all about it."

"You're a perfect tyrant!" cried Lady Caroline. "I'm ashamed of you, George; and I hope Claude will do exactly as he likes. *I* shall be sorry enough to lose him, goodness knows!"

"So shall I," said Olivia simply.

Lady Caroline shuddered.

"Look at the day!" cried Mr. Sellwood, jumping up with his pink face glowing beneath his virile silver hair. "Look at the sea! Look at the sand! Look at the sea-breeze lifting the very carpet under our feet! Was there ever such a day for golf?"

Claude wavered visibly.

"Come on," said Mr. Sellwood, catching up his clubs. "I'm awfully sorry for you, my boy. But come on!"

"You will have to give in, Claude," said Olivia, who loved her father.

Lady Caroline shrugged her shoulders.

"Of course," said she, "I hope he will; still I don't think our own selfish considerations should detain him against his better judgment."

"I am eager to see Cripps's partners," said Claude vacillating. "They may know more about it."

"And solicitors are such trying people," remarked Lady Caroline sympathetically; "one always does want to see them personally, to know what they really mean."

"That's what I feel," said Claude.

"But what on earth has he to consult them about?" demanded the Home Secretary. "Everything will keep — except the golf. Besides, my dear fellow, you are perfectly safe in the hands of Maitland, Hollis, Cripps and Company. A fine steady firm, and yet pushing too. I recollect they were the first solicitors in London —"

" Were ! " said his wife significantly.

" To supply us with typewritten briefs, my love. Now there is little else. In such hands, my dear Claude, your interests are quite un-dramatically safe."

" Still," said Claude, " it's an important matter; and I am, after all, for the moment, the head of —"

" I'll tell you what you are," cried the politician, with a burst of that hot brutality which had formerly made him the wholesome terror of the Junior Bar; " you're a confounded minor Cockney poet ! If you want to go back to your putrid midnight oil, go back to it; if you want to get out of the golf, get out of it ! I'm off. I shouldn't like to be rude to you, Claude, my boy, and I may be if I remain. No doubt I shall be able to pick up somebody down at the links."

Claude struck his flag.

A minute later, Olivia, from the broad bay window, watched the lank, handsome poet and the sturdy, white-haired statesman hurrying along the Marina arm-in-arm; both in knickerbockers and Norfolk jackets; and each carrying a quiverful of golf-clubs in his outer hand.

The girl was lost in thought.

"Olivia," said a voice behind her, "your father behaved like a brute!"

"I didn't think so; it was all in good part. And it will do him so much good!"

"Do whom?"

"Poor Claude! Of course he is dreadfully cut up."

"Then why did he pretend to be pleased?"

"That was his pluck. He took it splendidly. I never admired him so much!"

Lady Caroline opened her mouth to speak, but shut it again without a word. Her daughter's slight figure was silhouetted against the middle window of the bow; the sun put a golden crown upon the fair young head; yet the head was bent, and the girl's whole attitude one of pity and of thought. Lady Caroline Sellwood rose quietly, and left the room.

That species of low cunning, which was one of her Ladyship's traits, had placed her for the moment in a rather neat dilemma. Claude Lafont had cast poet's eyes at Olivia for months and years; and for weeks and months Olivia's mother had wished there were less poetry and more passion in the composition of that aristocrat. He would not say what nobody else, not even Lady Caroline, could say for him. He was content to dangle and admire; he had called Olivia his "faëry queen," with his lips and with his pen, in private and in print; but he had betrayed no immediate desire to call her his wife. Lady Caroline had recommended him to marry, and he had denounced marriage as "the death of romance." Quite sure in her own mind that she was dealing with none other than the Duke of St. Osmund's, it was her Ladyship who had planned the present small party (which her distinguished husband would call a "foursome") for the Easter Recess. Flatly disbelieving in the existence of the alleged Australian heir, she had seen the merit of engaging Olivia to Claude before the latter assumed his title in the eyes of the world. That the title was his to assume, when he liked, had been the opinion of all the Lafonts, save Claude himself, from the very first; and, when it suited her, Lady Caroline Sellwood was very well pleased to consider herself a Lafont. In point of fact, her mother had borne that illustrious name before her marriage with the impecunious Earl Clennell of Ballycawley; and Lady Caroline was herself a great-granddaughter of the sixth Duke of St. Osmund's.

The sixth Duke (who exerted himself to make the second half of the last century rather wickeder than the first) had two sons, of whom her present Ladyship's grandfather was the younger. The elder became the seventh Duke, and begot the eighth (and most respectable) Duke of St. Osmund's — the aged peer lately deceased. The eighth Duke, again, had but two sons, who both predeceased him. These two sons were, respectively, Claude's father and the unmentionable Marquis of Maske. The Marquis was a man after the heart of his worst ancestor, a fascinating blackguard, neither more nor less. At twenty-four he had raised the temperature of his native air to a degree incompatible with his own safety; and had fled the country never to return. Word of his death was received from Australia in the year 1866. He had died horribly, from thirst in the wilderness, and yet a proper compassion was impossible even after that. For the news was accompanied by a letter from the dead man's hand — scrawled at his last gasp, and pinned with his knife to the tree under which the body was found — yet composed in a vein of revolting cynicism, and containing further news of the most embarrassing description. The Marquis was leaving behind him — somewhere in Australia — at the moment he really could not say where — a small Viscount Dillamore to inherit ultimately the title and estates. He gave no dates, but said his wife was dead. To the best of his belief, however, the lad was alive; and might be known by the French eagle of the Lafonts, which the father had himself tattooed upon his little chest.

This was all the clue which had been left to Claude, to follow on a bad man's bare word, or to ignore at his own discretion. For reasons best known to himself, the old Duke had taken no steps to discover the little Marquis. Unluckily, however, his late Grace had not been entirely himself for many years before his death; and those reasons had never transpired. Claude, on the other hand, was a man of fastidious temperament, a person of infinite scruples, with a morbid horror of the incorrect. He would spend half the morning deciding between a semicolon and a full stop; and he was consistently conscientious in matters of real moment, as, for example, in that of his marriage. He had been asking himself, for quite a twelvemonth, whether he really loved Olivia; he had no intention of asking *her* until he was quite convinced on the point. To such a man there was but one course possible on the old Duke's death. And Claude had taken it with the worst results.

"He has no sympathy for *me*," said Lady Caroline bitterly, as she went upstairs. "He has cut his own throat, and there's an end of it; except that if he thinks he's going to marry any daughter of mine, after this, he is very much mistaken."

It was extremely mortifying all the same; to have prepared the ground so carefully, to have arranged every preliminary for a match which had now to be abandoned altogether; and worse still, to have turned away half the eligible young men in town for the sake of a Duke who was not a Duke at all. Lady Caroline Sellwood had three daughters. The eldest had made a good, solid, military marriage, and enjoyed in India a social position that was not unworthy of her. The second daughter had not done quite so well; still, her husband, the Rev. Francis Freke, was a divine whose birth was better than his attainments, so that there was every chance of seeing his little legs in gaiters before either foot was in his grave. But Olivia was her youngest ("my ewe lamb," Lady Caroline used to call her, although no other kind had graced her fold), and in her mother's opinion she was fitted for a better fate than that which had befallen either of her sisters. Olivia was the prettiest of the three. Her little fair head, "sunning over with curls," as Claude never tired of saying, was made by nature with a self-evident view to strawberry-leaves and twinkling tiaras. And Lady Caroline meant it to wear them yet.

She had done her best to encourage Claude in his inclination to run up to town at once. The situation at the seaside had become charged with danger. Not only did it appear to Lady Caroline that the poet was at last satisfied with the state of his own affections, but she had reason to fear that Claude Lafont would have a better chance with Olivia than would the Duke of St. Osmund's. The child was peculiar. She had read too much, and there was a suspiciously sentimental strain in her. Her acute mother did not imagine her " vulgarly in love " (as she called it) with the æsthetic Claude ; but she had heard him tell the girl that " pity from her " was " more dear than that from another "; and it was precisely this pity which Lady Caroline now dreaded as fervently as she would have welcomed it the day before. Her stupid husband had outwitted her in the matter of Claude's departure. Lady Caroline was hardly at the top of the stairs before she had made up the masterly mind which she considered at least a match for her stupid husband's. He would not allow her to get rid of Claude? Very well; nothing simpler. She would get rid of Olivia instead.

The means suggested itself almost as quickly as the end.

Lady Caroline took a little walk to the post-office, and said she had been on the pier. In a couple of hours a telegram arrived from Mrs. Freke, begging Olivia to go to her at once. Lady Caroline was apparently overwhelmed with surprise. But she despatched her ewe lamb by the next train.

"Olivia, I won both rounds!" called out the Home Secretary, when he strutted in towards evening, pink and beaming. Claude also looked the better and the brighter for his day; but Lady Caroline took the brightness out of him in an instant; and the Home Secretary beamed no more that night.

"It is no use your calling Olivia," said her Ladyship calmly; "by this time she must be a hundred miles away. You needn't look so startled, George. You know the state to which poor Francis reduces himself by the end of Lent, and you know that dear Mary's baby is not thriving as it ought. I shouldn't wonder if he makes *it* fast, too! At all events Mary telegraphed for Olivia this morning, and I let her go. Now it's no use being angry with any of us! With a young baby and a half-starved husband it was a very natural request. There's the telegram on the mantelpiece for you to see for yourself what she says."

CHAPTER II

"HAPPY JACK"

A DILETTANTE in letters, a laggard in love, and a pedant in much of his speech, Claude Lafont was nevertheless possessed of certain graces of the heart and head which entitled him at all events to the kindly consideration of his friends. He had enthusiasm and some soul; he had an open hand and an essentially simple mind. These were the merits of the man. They were less evident than his foibles, which, indeed, continually obscured them. He would have been the better for one really bad fault: but nature had not salted him with a single vice.

Unpopular at Eton, he had found his feet perhaps a little too firmly at Oxford. There his hair had grown long and his views outrageous. Had the old Duke of St. Osmund's been in his right mind at the time, he would certainly have quitted it at the report of some of his grandson's contributions to the university debates. Claude, however, had the courage of his most extravagant opinions, and even at Oxford he was a man whom it was possible to respect. The era of Toynbee Hall and a gentlemanly, kid-gloved Socialism came a little later; there were other and intermediate phases, into which it is unnecessary to enter. Claude came through them all with two things, at least, as good as new: ·his ready enthusiasm and his excellent heart.

Whether he really did view the new twist in his life with the satisfaction which he professed is an open and immaterial question; all that is certain or important is the fact that he did not permit himself to repine. He was never in better spirits than in the six weeks’ interval between the receipt of Mr. Cripps’s cable and that gentleman’s arrival with the new Duke. Claude divided the time between the proofs of his new volume of poems and conscientious preparations for the proper reception of his noble cousin. He had the mansion in Belgrave Square, which had fallen of late years into disuse, elaborately done up, repapered, and fitted throughout with new hangings and the electric light. He felt it his duty to hand over the house in a cleanly and habitable state; and he was accustomed to work his duty rather hard.

He ran down to Maske Towers, the principal
family seat, repeatedly, and had certain renova-
tions carried out as far as possible under his
own eye. In every direction he did more than
he need have done. And so the time passed
very busily, quite happily, and with an interest
that was kept green to the last by the utter
absence of any shred of information concerning
the ninth Duke of St. Osmund's.

Claude had even no idea as to whether he
was a married man. So he legislated for a wife
and family. And his worst visions were of a
hulking, genial, sheep-farming Duke, with a
tribe of very terrible little Lords and Ladies,
duly frightened of their gigantic father, but
paying not the slightest attention to the anæmic
Duchess who all day scolded them through her
freckled nose.

Mr. Cripps's letters continued to arrive by
each week's mail; but they were still written
with a shake of the head and a growing depre-
cation of the wild-goose chase in which the
lawyer now believed himself to be unworthily
engaged. Towards the end of May, however,
the letters stopped. The last one was written
on the eve of an expedition up the country, on
a mere off-chance, to find out more about one
John Dillamore, whom Mr. Cripps had heard of

as a resident of the Riverina. Claude Lafont knew well what had come of that off-chance. It had turned the tide of his life. But no letter came from the Riverina; the next communication was a telegram from Brindisi, saying they had left the ship and were travelling overland; and the next after that, another telegram stating the hour at which they hoped to land at Dover.

Claude Lafont had just time enough to put on his hat, to stop the hansom for an instant at the house in Belgrave Square, and to catch the 12.0 from Victoria.

It was a lovely day in early June. There was neither a cloud in the sky nor the white crest of a wave out at sea; the one was as serenely blue as the other; and the *Calais-Douvre* rode in with a high-bred calm and dignity all in key with the occasion. Claude boarded her before he had any right, with a sudden dereliction of his characteristic caution. And there was old Cripps, sunburnt and grim, with a soft felt hat on his head, and a strange spasmodic twitching at the corners of the mouth.

"Here you are!" cried Claude, gripping hands. "Well, where is he?"

The lawyer's lips went in and out, and a rough-looking bystander chuckled audibly.

"One thing quickly," whispered Claude: "is he a married man?"

"No, he isn't."

The bystander laughed outright. Claude favoured him with a haughty glance.

"His servant, I presume?"

"No," said Cripps hoarsely. "I must introduce you. The Duke of St. Osmund's — your kinsman, Mr. Claude Lafont."

Claude felt the painful pressure of a horny fist, and gasped.

"Proud to meet you, mister," said the Duke.

"So delighted to meet and welcome *you*, Duke," said Claude faintly.

"I'm afraid I'm a bit of a larrikin," continued the Duke. "You'd have done as well to leave me where I was — but now I'm here you've got to call me Jack."

"You knew, of course, what would happen sooner or later?" said Claude, with a sickly smile.

"Not me. My colonial oath, I did *not!* Never dreamt of it till I seen *him*" — with a jerk of his wideawake towards Mr. Cripps. It was a very different felt hat from that gentleman's; the crown rose like a sugar-loaf, nine inches from the head; the brim was nearly as many inches wide; and where the felt touched

the temples it was stained through and through
with ancient perspiration.

"And I can't sight it now!" added his Grace.

"Nevertheless it's true," said Mr. Cripps.

Claude was taking in the matted beard, the
peeled nose, and the round shoulders of the
ninth Duke. He was a bushman from top to toe.

"What luggage have you?" exclaimed Claude,
with a sudden effort. "We must get it ashore."

"This is all," said the Duke, with a grin.

It lay on the deck at their feet: a long cylin-
der whose outer case was an old blue blanket,
very neatly rolled and strapped; an Australian
saddle, with enormous knee-pads, black with
age; and an extraordinary cage like a rabbit-
hutch. The cage was full of cats. The Duke
insisted on carrying it ashore himself.

"This *is* the man?" whispered Claude, jeal-
ously, to Mr. Cripps.

"The man himself; there's an eagle on his
chest as large as life."

"But it might be a coincidence —— "

"It might be, but it isn't," replied Cripps
shortly. "He's the Duke all right; the papers
I shall show you are quite conclusive. I own
he doesn't look the part. He's not tractable.
He would come as he is. I heaved one old hat
overboard; but he had a worse in his swag.

However, no one on board knew who he was. I took care of that."

"God bless you, Cripps!" said Claude Lafont.

He had reserved a first-class carriage. The Duke took up half of it with his cat-cage, which he stoutly declined to trust out of his sight. There were still a few minutes before the train would start. Claude and Cripps exchanged sympathetic glances.

"I think we ought to drink the Duke's health," said Claude, who for once felt the need of a stimulant himself.

"I think so too," said Mr. Cripps.

"Then make 'em lock the door," stipulated his Grace. "I wouldn't risk my cats being shook, not for drinks as long as your leg!"

A grinning guard came forward with his key. The Duke "mistered" him, and mentioned where his cats came from as he got out.

"Very kind of you to shout for me," he continued as they filed into the refreshment room; "but why the blazes don't you call me Jack? Happy Jack's my name, that's what they used to call me up the bush. I'm not going to stop being Jack, or happy either, 'cause I'm a Dook; if I did I'd jolly soon sling it. Now, my dear, what are you givin' us? Why don't you let me help myself, like they do up the bush? English fashion, is it? And you call that drop a nobbler, do you, in the old country? Well, well, here's fun!"

The Duke's custodians were not sorry to get him back beside his cats. They were really glad when the train started. The Duke was in high spirits. The whisky had loosened his tongue.

"Like cats, old man?" he inquired of Claude. "Then I hope you'll make friends with mine. They were my only mates, year in, year out, up at the hut. I wasn't going to leave 'em there when they'd stood by me so long; not likely; so here they are. See that black 'un in the corner? I call her Black Maria, and that's her kitten. She went and had a large family at sea, but this poor little beggar's the only one what lived to tell the tale. That great big Tom, he's the father. I don't think much of Tom, but it would have been a shame to leave him behind. No, sir, my favourite's the little tortoise-shell with the game leg. He got cotched in a rabbit trap last shearing-time; he's the most adventurous little cat that ever was, so I call him Livingstone. I've known him explore five miles from the hut, when there wasn't a drop of water or a blade of feed in the paddicks, and yet come back as fat as butter. A little caution, I tell you! Out you come, Livingstone!"

Claude thought he had never seen a more ill-favoured animal. To call it tortoise-shell was to misuse the word. It was simply yellow; it ran on three legs; and its nose had been recently scarified by an enemy's claws.

"No, I'm full up of Tom," pursued the Duke, fondling his pet. "Look what he done on board to Livingstone's nose! I nearly slung him over the side. Poor little puss, then, poor little puss! You may well purr, old toucher; there's a live Lord scratching your head."

"Meaning me?" said Claude genially; there was a kindness in the rugged face, as it bent over the little yellow horror, that appealed to the poet.

"Meaning you, of course."

"But I'm not one."

"You're not? What a darned shame! Why, you ought to be a Dook. You'd make a better one than me!"

The family solicitor was half-hidden behind that morning's *Times;* as Jack spoke, he hid himself entirely. Claude, for his part, saw nothing to laugh at. The Duke's face was earnest. The Duke's eyes were dark and kind. Like Claude himself, he had the long Lafont nose, though sun and wind had peeled it red; and a pair of shaggy brown eyebrows gave strength at all events to the hairy face. Claude was thinking that half-an-hour at Truefitt's, a pot of vaseline, and the best attentions of his own tailors in Maddox Street would make a new man of Happy Jack. Not that his suit was on a par with his abominable wideawake. He could not have worn these clothes in the bush. They were obviously his best; and, as obviously, ready-made.

Happy Jack was meantime apostrophising his pet.

"Ah! but you was with me when that there gentleman found me, wasn't you, Livingstone? You should tell the other gentleman about that. We never thought we was a Dook, did we? We thought ourselves a blooming ordinary common man. My colonial oath, and so we are! But you recollect that last bu'st of ours, Livingstone? I mean the time we went to knock down the thirty-one pound cheque what never got knocked down properly at all. We had a rare thirst on us ——"

Mr. Cripps in his corner smacked down the *Times* on his knees.

"Look there!" he cried. "Did ever you see such grass as that, Jack? You've nothing like it in New South Wales. I declare it does my old heart good to see an honest green field again!"

Jack looked out for an instant only.

"Ten sheep to the acre," said he. "Wonderful, isn't it, Livingstone? And you an' me used to ten acres to the sheep! But we were talking about that last little spree; you want your Uncle Claude to hear all about it, I see you do; you're not the cat to make yourself out better than what you are; not you, Livingstone! Well, as I was saying——"

"Those red-tiled roofs are simply charming!" exclaimed the solicitor.

"A perfect poem," said Claude.

"And that May-tree in full bloom!"

"A living lyric," said Claude.

It was really apple-blossom.

"And you," cried the Duke to his cat, "you're a comic song, that's what *you* are! Tell 'em you won't be talked down, Livingstone. Tell this gentleman he's got to hear the worst. Tell him that when the other gentleman found us"—the solicitor raised his *Times* with a shrug—"one of us was drunk, drunk, drunk; and the other was watching over him—and the other was my little cat!"

"You're joking, of course?" said Claude, with a flush.

"Not me, mister. That's a fact. You see, it was like this——"

"Thanks," said Claude hastily; "but I'd far rather not know."

"Why not, old toucher?"

"It would hurt me," said Claude, with a shudder.

"Hurt you! Hear that, Livingstone? It would hurt him to hear how we knocked down our last little cheque! That's the best one *I*'ve heard since I left the ship!"

"Nevertheless it's the case."

"And do you mean to tell me you were never like that yourself?"

"Never in my life."

"Well, shoot me dead!" whispered the Duke in his amazement.

"It ought not to surprise you," said Claude, in a tone that set the *Times* shaking in the far corner of the carriage.

"It does, though. I can't help it. You're the first I've ever met that could say as much."

"Pray let us drop the subject. I prefer to hear no more. You pain me more than I can say!"

Claude's flush had deepened; his supersensitive soul was indeed scandalised, and so visibly that an answering flush showed upon the Duke's mahogany features, like an extra coat of polish.

"I pain you!" he echoed, dropping his cat.

"I'm very sorry then. I am so! I had no intention of doing any such thing. All I wanted was to fly my true flag at once, like, and have done with it. And I've pained you; and you bet I'll go on paining you all the time! How can I help it? I'm not what us back-blockers call a parlour-man, though I may be a Dook; but neither the one nor the other is my fault. You should have let me be in the bush. I was all right there — all right with my hut and my cats. I'd never known anything better. I never knew who I was. What did it matter if I knocked down my cheque when I got full up of the cats and the hut? Nobody thinks anything of that up the bush. The boss used always to take me on again; some day I'll tell you about my old boss; he was the best friend ever I had. A real gentleman, who thought no worse of you so long's it only happened now and then. But see here! It shall never happen again. It didn't matter in the boundary rider, but p'r'aps it might in the Dook. Anyhow I'm strict T T from this moment; that whisky at Dover shall be my last. And I'm darned sorry I pained you, and — and dash it, here's my fist on it for good and all!"

It is difficult to say which hand wrung the harder. Claude was not pleased with himself;

the conscious lack of some quality, which the other possessed, was afflicting him with a novel and entirely unexpected sense of inferiority. He was as yet unsure what the missing quality was; he hardly suspected it of being a virtue; but it was new to Claude to have these feelings at all.

He said not another word upon the embarrassing subject, but fell presently into a train of thought that kept him silent until they steamed into Victoria. There the conquering Cripps was met by his wife and daughters; but Claude managed to get a few more words with him as they were waiting to have the baggage passed.

“I like him,” said Claude.

“So do I,” was the reply, “and I know him well.”

“I like his honesty.”

“He is honesty itself. I did my best just now to keep him from giving himself away — but that was his deliberate game. Mark you, what he insisted on telling you was quite true; but on the whole he has behaved excellently ever since.”

“Well, as long as he doesn’t confess his sins to everybody he meets!”

“No fear of that; he looks on you as still the head of the family, with a sort of *ex officio* right to know the worst. His own position he doesn’t

realise a bit.   Yet some day I expect to see him
at least as fit to occupy it as one or two others;
and you are the man to make him so.   You will
only require two things."

The great doors opened inwards, and the
travellers surged in to claim their luggage, with
Mr. Cripps at their head.   Claude caught him
by the elbow as he was pointing out his trunks.

" Those two things ? " said he.

" Yes, those two, with my initials on each."

" No, but the two things that I shall need?"

" Oh, those !   Plenty of patience, and plenty
of time."

CHAPTER III

A CHANCE LOST

IT was the pink of the evening when the
cousins drove off in a four-wheeler with the
cats on top. Claude had been in many minds
about their destination, until the Duke had
asked him to recommend an hotel. At that he
had hesitated a little, and finally pitched upon
the First Avenue. A variety of feelings guided
his choice, chief among them being a vague impression that his wild kinsman would provoke
less attention in Holborn than in Northumber-
land Avenue. To Holborn, at all events, they
were now on their way.

Claude sat far back in the cab; he felt thankful it was not a hansom. In the Mall they met
a string of them, taking cloaked women and
white-breasted men out to dinner. Claude saw
one or two faces he knew, but was himself unseen. He saw them stare and smile at the
tanned and bearded visage beneath that vil-
lainous wideawake, which was thrust from one

window to the other with the eager and unrestrained excitement of a child. He felt ashamed of poor Jack. He was sincerely ashamed of this very feeling.

"What streets!" whispered the Duke in an awestruck whisper. "We've nothing like 'em in Melbourne. They'd knock spots off Sydney. I've been in both."

Claude had a sudden thought. "For you," he said, "these streets should have a special interest."

"How's that?"

"Well, many of them belong to you."

"WHAT?"

"You are the ground landlord of some of the streets and squares we have already passed."

The brown beard had fallen in dismay; now, however, a mouthful of good teeth showed themselves in a frankly incredulous grin.

"What are you givin' us?" laughed Jack. "I see, you think you've got a loan of a new chum! Well, so you have. Go ahead!"

"Not if you don't choose to believe me," replied Claude stiffly. "I meant what I said; I usually do. The property has been in our family for hundreds of years."

"And now it's mine?"

"And now it's yours."

The Duke of St. Osmund's took off his monstrous wideawake, and passed the back of his hairy hand across his forehead. The gesture was eloquent of a mind appalled.

"Have I no homestead on my own run?" he inquired at length.

"You have several," said Claude, smiling; but he also hesitated.

"Several in London?" cried the Duke, aghast again.

"No — only one in town."

"That's better! I say, though, why aren't we going there?"

"Well, the fact is, they're not quite ready for you; I mean the servants. They — we were all rather rushed, you know, and they don't expect you to-night. Do you mind?"

Claude had stated but one fact of many. That morning, when he stopped his hansom at the house, he had told the servants not to expect his Grace until he telegraphed. After seeing the Duke, he had resolved not to telegraph at all; and certainly not to install him in his own house, as he was, without consulting other members of the family. He still considered that decision justified. Nevertheless, the Duke's reply came as a great relief.

"No, I'm just as glad," said Jack content-

edly. His contentment was only comparative,
however. The first dim conception of his great-
ness had strangely dashed him; he was no
longer the man that he had been in the train.

An athlete in a frayed frock-coat, and no
shirt, was sprinting behind the cab with the
customary intent; it was a glimpse of him, as
they turned a corner, that slew the oppressed
Duke, and brought Happy Jack back to life.

"Stop the cab!" he roared; "there's a man
on the track of my cats!"

"Nonsense, my dear fellow; it's only a person who'll want sixpence for not helping with
the luggage."

"Are you sure?" asked Jack suspiciously.
"How do you know he isn't a professional cat-
stealer? I must ask the cabman if they are all
right!" He did so, and was reassured.

"We're almost at the hotel now," said Claude,
with misgivings; he was bitterly anticipating
the sensation to be caused there by the arrival
of such a Duke of St. Osmund's, and wondering whether it would be of any use suggesting
a further period of *incognito*.

"Nearly there, are we? Then see here," said
Jack, "I've got something to insist on. I mean
to have my way about one matter."

Claude groaned inwardly.

"What is it?" he asked.

"I'll tell you straight. I'm not going to do the Dook in this hotel. I'm plain Jack Dillamore, or I don't go in."

The delight of this deliverance nearly overcame the poet.

"I think you're wise," was all he trusted himself to say. "I should be inclined to take the same course were I in your place. You will escape a great deal of the sort of adulation which turneth the soul sick. And for one night, at all events, you will be able, as an alien outsider, to form an unprejudiced opinion of our unlovely metropolis."

In the bright light of his ineffable relief, Claude's little mannerisms stood out once more, like shadows when the sun shines fitfully; but it was a transient gleam. The arrival at the hotel was still embarrassing enough. The wide-awake attracted attention. The attention was neither of a flattering character in itself nor otherwise desirable from any point of view. It made Claude miserable. There was also trouble about the cats.

Jack insisted on having them with him in his room. The management demurred. Jack threatened to go elsewhere. The management raised no objection; but Claude did. He handed them his card, and this settled the matter. There is but one race of Lafonts in England. So Jack had his way. A room was taken; the cats were put into it; milk was set before them; and Jack left the hotel in Claude's company, with the key of that room in his pocket.

Claude would have taken him to his club, but for both their sakes he did not dare. Yet he was as anxious as ever to show every hospitality to the Duke. Accordingly he had refused Jack's invitation to dine with him in the hotel, and was taking him across to the Holborn instead.

The dinner went wonderfully. Jack was delighted with the music, with the electric lights, with the marble pillars, with the gilded balconies, with the dinner itself, in fact with everything. There was but one item which did not appeal to him: he stoutly refused to drink a drop of wine.

"A promise is a promise," said he. "I gave you my colonial in the train, and I mean to keep it; for a bit, at all events."

Claude protested and tempted him in vain. Jack called for a lemon-squash, and turned his wine-glasses upside down. He revenged himself, however, upon the viands.

"Which *entrée*, please, sir?" said the waiter.

“Both!” cried Jack. “You may go on, mister, till I tell you to stop!”

After dinner the cousins went aloft, and Claude took out his cigarette case and ordered cigars for the Duke. He could not smoke them himself, but neither, it appeared, could Jack. *He* produced a cutty-pipe, black and foul with age, and a cake of tobacco like a piece of shoe-leather, which he began paring with his knife. Claude had soon to sit farther away from him.

Jack did not fancy a theatre; he was strongly in favour of a quiet evening and a long talk; and it was he who proposed that they should return, for this purpose, to the First Avenue. No sooner were they comfortably settled in the hotel smoking-room, however, than the Duke announced that he must run upstairs and see to his cats. And he came down no more that night.

Claude waited patiently for twenty minutes. Then he began a note to Lady Caroline Sellwood. Then he remembered that he could, if he liked, see Lady Caroline that night. It was merely a question of driving over to his rooms in St. James's and putting himself into evening dress. On the whole, this seemed worth doing. Claude therefore followed Jack upstairs after an interval of half-an-hour.

The Duke's rooms were on the first floor. Claude surprised a group of first-floor servants laughing and whispering in the corridor. The little that he heard as he passed made him hot all over. The exact words were:

"Never see such a man in my life." "Nor me, my dear!" "And yet they call this 'ere a decent 'otel!"

Claude had no doubt in his own mind as to whom they were talking about. Already the Duke inspired him with a sort of second-self-consciousness. Prepared for anything, he hastened to the room and nervously knocked at the door.

"Come in!" cried Jack's voice.

The door was unlocked; as Claude opened it the heat of the room fairly staggered him. It was a sufficiently warm summer night, yet an enormous fire was burning in the grate.

"My *dear* fellow!" panted Claude.

Jack was in his trousers and shirt; the sleeves were rolled up over his brawny arms; the open front revealed an estuary of hairy chest; and it was plain at a glance that the Duke was perspiring at every pore.

"It's all right," he said. "It's for the cats."

"The cats!" said Claude. They were lying round about the fire.

“ Yes, poor devils! They had a fire every day in the hut, summer and winter. They never had a single one at sea. They like to sleep by it — they always did — all but Livingstone. He sleeps with me when he isn’t on the loose.”

“ But you’ll never be able to sleep in an atmosphere like this! ”

Jack was cutting up a pipeful of his black tobacco.

“ Well, it *is* warm,” he admitted. “ And now you mention it, I may find it a job to get asleep; but the cats like it, anyhow! ” And he swore at them affectionately as he lit his pipe.

“ Did you forget you’d left me downstairs? ” asked Claude.

“ Clean! I apologise. I took this idea into my head, and I could think of nothing else.”

“ May we have another window open? Thank you. I’ll smoke one cigarette; then I must be off.”

“ Where to ? ”

“ My chambers — to dress.”

“ To *undress*, you mean! ”

“ No, to dress. I’ve got to go out to a — to a party. I had almost forgotten about it. The truth is, I want to see Lady Caroline Sellwood,

who, although not a near relation, is about the
only woman in London with our blood in her
veins. She will want to see you. What's the
matter?"

Jack's pipe had gone out in his hand; and
there he stood, a pillar of perspiring bewilder-
ment.

"A party!" he murmured. "At this time
o' night!"

Claude laughed.

"It's not ten o'clock yet; if I'm there before
half-past eleven I shall be too early."

"I give you best," said Jack, shaking his
head, and putting another light to his pipe.
"It licks *me!* Who's the madman who gives
parties in the middle of the night?"

"My dear fellow, everybody does! In this
case it's a woman: the Countess of Darlingford."

"A live Countess!"

"Well, but you're a live Duke."

"But—I'm—a live—Dook!"

Jack repeated the words as though the fact
had momentarily escaped him. His pipe went
out again. This time he made no attempt to
relight it, but stood staring at Claude with his
bare brown arms akimbo, and much trouble in
his rugged, honest face.

"You can't get out of it," laughed Claude.

"I can!" he cried. "I mean to get out of it! I'm not the man for the billet. I wasn't dragged up to it. And I don't want it! I shall only make a darned ass of myself and everybody else mixed up with me. I may be the man by birth, but I'm not the man by anything else; and look here, I want to back out of it while there's time; and you're the very man to help me. I wasn't dragged up to it — but you were. I'm not the man for the billet — but you are. The very man! You go to parties in the middle of the night, and you think nothing of 'em. They'd be the death of Happy Jack! The whole thing turns me sick with funk — the life, the money, the responsibility. I never got a sight of it till to-day; and now I don't want it at any price. You'd have got it if it hadn't been for me; so take it now — for God's sake, take it now! If it's mine, it's mine to give. I give it to you! Claude, old toucher, be the Dook yourself. Let me and the cats clear back to the bush!"

The poet had listened with amazement, with amusement, with compassion and concern. He now shook his head.

"You ask an impossibility. Without going into the thing, take my word for it that what you propose is utterly and hopelessly out of the question."

"Couldn't I disappear?" said Jack eagerly. "Couldn't I do a bolt in the night? It's a big chance for you; surely you won't lose it by refusing to help me clear out?"

Claude again shook his head.

"In a week's time you will be laughing at what you are saying now. You are one of the richest men in England; everything that money can buy you can have. You own some of the loveliest seats in the whole country; wait till I have shown you Maske Towers! You won't want to clear out then. You won't ask me to be the Duke again!"

He had purposely dwelt upon those material allurements which the bushman's mind would most readily grasp. And it was obvious that his arguments had hit the target, although not, perhaps, the bull's-eye.

"Anyhow," said Jack doggedly, "it's an offer! And I repeat it. What's more, I mean it too!"

"Then I decline it," returned Claude, to humour him; "and there's an end of the matter. Look here, though. One thing I promise. If you like, I'll see you through!"

"You will?"

"I will with all my heart."

"And you're quite sure you won't take on the whole show yourself?"

"Quite sure," said Claude, smiling.

"Still, you'll tell me what to do? You'll tell me what not to do? You'll show me the ropes? You'll have hold of my sleeve?"

"I'll do all that; at least, I'll do all I can. It may not be much. Still I'll do it."

Jack held out a hot, damp hand; yet, just then, he seemed to be perspiring most freely under the eyes.

"You're a good sort, Claudy!" said he hoarsely.

"Good-night, old fellow," said Claude Lafont.

CHAPTER IV

NOT IN THE PROGRAMME

LADY CAROLINE SELLWOOD'S incomparable
Wednesdays were so salient a feature of those
seasons during which her husband was in office,
and her town house in St. James's Square, that
their standard is still quoted as the ideal of its
kind. These afternoons were never dull. Lady
Caroline cast a broad net, and her average
draught included representatives of every decent
section of the community. But she also possessed some secret recipe, the envy and the despair of other professional hostesses, and in her
rooms there was never an undue preponderance
of any one social ingredient. Every class—
above a certain line, not drawn too high—was
represented; none was over done; nor was the
mistake made of "packing" the assembly with
interesting people. The very necessary comple-
ment of the merely interested was never wanting.
One met beauty as well as brains; wealth as
well as wit; and quite as many colourless non-

entities as notorieties of every hue. The proportion was always perfect, but not more so than
the general good-temper of the guests. They
foregathered like long-lost brothers and sisters:
the demagogue and the divine; the judge and
the junior; the oldest lady and the newest
woman; the amateur playwright and the actor-
manager who had lost his play; the minor
novelist and the young lady who had never
heard of him; and my Lords and Ladies (whose
carriages half-filled the Square) with the very
least of these. It was wonderful to see them
together; it was a solemn thought, but yet a
fact, that their heavenly behaviour was due
simply and entirely to the administrative genius
of Lady Caroline Sellwood.

The Home Secretary hated the Wednesdays;
he was the one person who did; and *he* only
hated them because they *were* Wednesdays —
and from the period of his elderly infatuation
for golf. It was his great day for a round; and
Lady Caroline had to make his excuses every
week when it was fine. This was another thing
which her Ladyship did beautifully. She would
say, with a voice full of sympathy, equally
divided between those mutual losers, her guest
and her husband, that poor dear George had to
address such and such a tiresome deputation;

when, as a matter of fact, he was "addressing" his golf-ball on Wimbledon Common, and enjoying himself exceedingly. Now, among other Wednesdays, the Home Secretary was down at Wimbledon (with a prominent member of the Opposition) on the afternoon following the arrival in London of the ninth Duke of St. Osmund's; and Mr. Sellwood never knew whether to pity his wife, or to congratulate himself, on his absence from her side on that occasion.

One of their constant ornaments, Claude Lafont, had been forced to eschew these Wednesdays of late weeks. Lady Caroline Sellwood had never been quite the same to him since the Easter Recess. She had treated him from that time with a studied coolness quite inexplicable to his simple mind; and finally, at Lady Darlingford's, she had been positively rude. Claude, of course, had gone there expressly to prepare Lady Caroline for the new Duke. This he conceived to be his immediate duty, and he attempted to perform it, in the kindliest spirit imaginable, with all the tact at his command. Lady Caroline declined to hear him out. She chose to put a sinister construction upon his well-meant words, and to interrupt them with the announcement that she intended, with Claude's permission, to judge the Duke for herself. Was he married? Ha! then where was he to be found? Claude told her, was coldly thanked, and went home to writhe all that Tuesday night under the mortification of his kinswoman's snub.

Yet, on the Wednesday afternoon, Claude Lafont not only went to the Sellwoods' as though nothing had happened, but he was there before the time. And Lady Caroline was not only amazed, but (for the first time since Easter) really pleased to see him: for already she had been given cause to regret her insolent disregard of him overnight at Lady Darlingford's. She was even composing an apology when the whiteness of Claude's face brought her thoughts to a standstill.

"Have you seen him?" he cried, as they met.

"The Duke?"

"Yes — haven't you seen him this morning?"

"No, indeed! Haven't you?"

Claude sat down with a groan, shaking his head, and never seeing the glittering, plump, outstretched hand.

"Haven't you?" repeated Lady Caroline, sitting down herself.

"Not this morning. I made sure he would come here!"

"So he ought to have done. I asked him to lunch. The note was written and posted the instant we came in from the Darlingfords'. Claude, I wasn't nice to you there! Can you forgive me? I thought you were prejudiced. My dreadful temper rose in arms on the side of the absent man; it always was my great weakness rightly or wrongly to take the part of those who aren't there to stick up for themselves!"

Her great weakness was of quite another character, but Claude bowed. He was barely listening.

"I've lost him," he said, looking at Lady Caroline, with a rolling eye. "He's disappeared."

"Never!"

"This morning," said Claude. "I did so hope he was here!"

"He sent no answer, not one word, and he never came. Who saw him last?"

"The hotel people, early this morning. It seems he ordered a horse for seven o'clock, shortly after I left him last night. So they got him one, and off he went before breakfast in the flannel collar and the outrageous bush wideawake in which he landed. And he's never come back."

A change came over Lady Caroline Sellwood. She drew her chair a little nearer, and she favoured Claude Lafont with a kindlier glance than he had had from her since Easter.

"Something may have happened," whispered Lady Caroline hopefully.

"That's just it. Something *must* have happened."

"But something dreadful! Only last season there was a man killed in the Row! Was he — a *very* rough diamond, Claude?"

"Very."

Lady Caroline sighed complacently.

"But you can't help liking him," hastily added Claude, "and I hope to goodness nothing serious is the matter!"

"Of course, so do I. That goes without saying."

"Nor is he at all a likely man to be thrown. He has lived his life in the saddle. By the way, he brought his own old bush-saddle with him, and it appears that he insisted on riding out in that too."

"You see, Claude, it's a pity you didn't leave him in the bush; he's evidently devoted to it still."

"He is — that's the trouble; he has already spoken of bolting back there. My fear is that he may even now be suiting the action to the word."

"Don't tell me that," said Lady Caroline, whose head was still full of her first theory.

"It's what I fear; he's just the sort of fellow to go back by the first boat, if the panic took him.   He showed signs of a panic last night. You see, he's only just beginning to realise what his position here will mean.   And it frightens him; it may have frightened him out of our sight once and for all."

Lady Caroline shook her head.

"My fear is that he has broken his neck! And if he has, depend upon it, sad as it would be, it would still be for the best.   That's what I always say: everything is for the best," repeated Lady Caroline, pensively gazing at Claude's handsome head.   "However," she added, as the door opened, "here's Olivia; go and ask her what she thinks.   *I* am prepared for the worst.   And pray stop, dear Claude, and let us talk the matter over after the others have gone.   We may *know* the worst by that time.   And we have seen nothing of you this season!"

Olivia looked charming.   She was also kind to Claude.   But she entirely declined to embrace her mother's dark view of the Duke's disappearance. On the other hand, she was inconveniently inquisitive about his looks and personality, and Claude had to say many words for his cousin before he could get in one for himself. However, he did at length contrive to speak of his new volume of poems. It was just out. He was having a copy of the exceedingly limited large-paper edition specially bound in vellum for Olivia's acceptance. Olivia seemed pleased, and apart from his anxiety Claude had not felt so happy for weeks. They were allowed to talk to each other until the rooms began to fill.

It was a very good Wednesday; but then the season was at its height. The gathering comprised the usual measure of interesting and interested persons, and the former had made their names upon as many different fields as ever. Claude had a chat with his friend, Edmund Stubbs, a young man with an unhealthy skin and a vague reputation for immense cleverness. They spoke of the poems. Stubbs expressed a wish to see the large-paper edition, which was not yet for sale, as did Ivor Llewellyn, the impressionist artist, who was responsible for the "decorations" in most volumes of contemporary minor verse, Claude's included. Claude was injudicious enough to invite both men to his rooms that night. The Impressionist was the most remarkable-looking of all Lady Caroline's guests. He wore a curled fringe and a flowing tie, and pince-nez attached to his person by a broad black ribbon. His pale face was prematurely drawn, and he showed his gums in a deathly grin at the many hard things which Stubbs muttered at the expense of all present whom he knew by sight. Claude had a high opinion of both these men, but for once he was scarcely in tune for their talk, which was ever at a sort of artistic-intellectual concert-pitch. The Duke was to be forgotten in the society of Olivia only. Claude therefore edged away, trod on the skirts of a titled divorcée, got jammed between an Irish member and a composer of comic songs, and was finally engaged in conversation by the aged police magistrate, Sir Joseph Todd.

Sir Joseph had lowered his elephantine form into a chair beside the tea-table, where he sat, with his great cane between his enormous legs, munching cake like a school-boy and winking at his friends. He winked at Claude. The magistrate had been a journalist, and a scandalous Bohemian, so he said, in his young days; he had given Claude introductions and advice when the latter took to his pen. He, also, inquired after the new book, but rather grimly, and expressed himself with the rough edge of his tongue on the subject of modern "poets" and "poetry": the inverted commas were in his voice.

"You young spring poets," said he, "are too tender by half; you're all white meat together. You may say that's no reason why I should have my knife in you. Why didn't you say it? A bad joke would be a positive treat from you precious young fellows of to-day. And you give us bad lyrics instead, in limited editions; that's the way it takes you now."

Claude laughed; he was absurdly good-humoured under hostile criticism, a quality of which some of his literary friends were apt to take advantage. On this occasion, however, his unconcern was partly due to inattention. While listening to his old friend he was thinking still of the Duke.

"I'm sorry you would be a poet, Claude," the magistrate continued. "The price of poets has gone down since my day. And you'd have done so much better in the House — by which, of course, I mean the House we all thought you were bound for. Has he — has he turned up yet?"

"Oh yes; he's in England," replied Claude, with discretion.

Sir Joseph pricked his ears, but curbed his tongue. Of all the questions that gathered on his lips, only one was admissible, even in so old a friend as himself.

"A family man?"

"No; a bachelor."

"Capital! We shall see some fun, eh?" chuckled Sir Joseph, gobbling the last of his last slice. "What a quarry—what a prize! I was reminded of him only this morning, Claude. I had an Australian up before me— a most astounding fellow! An escaped bush-ranger, I should call him; looked as if he'd been cut straight out of a penny dreadful; never saw such a man in my life. However——"

Claude was not listening; his preoccupation was this time palpable. The mouth of him was open, and his eyes were fixed; the police magistrate followed their lead, with double eye-glasses in thick gold frames; and then *his* mouth opened too.

Her guests were making way for Lady Caroline Sellwood, who was leading towards the tea-table, by his horny hand, none other than the ninth Duke of St. Osmund's himself. Her Ladyship's face was radiant with smiles; yet the Duke was just as he had been the day before, as unkempt, as undressed (his Crimean shirt had a flannel collar, but no tie), as round-shouldered; with his nose and ears still flayed by the sun; and the notorious wideawake tucked under his arm.

"He has come straight from the bush," her Ladyship informed everybody (as though she meant some shrub in the Square garden), "and just as he is. I call it so sweet of him! You know you'll never look so picturesque again, my dear Duke!"

Olivia followed with the best expression her frank face could muster. Claude took his cousin's hand in a sudden hush.

"Where in the world have you been?" broke from him before them all.

"Been? I've been run in," replied the Duke, with a smack of his bearded grinning lips.

"Tea or coffee, Duke?" said Lady Caroline, all smiling tolerance. "Tea? A cup of tea for the Duke of St. Osmund's. And *where* do you say you have been?"

"Locked up!" said his Grace. "In choky, if you like it better!"

Lady Caroline herself led the laugh. The situation was indeed worthy of her finely tempered steel, her consummate tact, her instinctive dexterity. Many a grander dame would have essayed to quell that incriminating tongue. Not so Lady Caroline Sellwood. She took her Australian wild bull very boldly by the horns.

"I do believe," she cried, "that you are what we have all of us been looking for — in real life — all our days. I do believe you are the shocking Duke of those dreadful melodramas in the flesh at last! What was your crime? Ah! I've no doubt you cannot tell us!"

"Can I not?" cried the Duke, as Claude stopped him, unobserved, from pouring his tea into the saucer. "I'll tell you all about it, and perhaps you'll show me where the crime comes in, for I'm bothered if I see it yet. All I did was to have a gallop along one of your streets; I don't even know which street it was; but there's a round clearing at one end, then a curve, and then another clearing at the far end."

"Regent Street," murmured Claude.

"That's the name. Well, it was quite early, there was hardly anybody about, so I thought surely to goodness there could be no harm in a gallop; and I had one from clearing to clearing. Blowed if they didn't run me in for that!

They kept me locked up all the morning. Then they took me before a fat old joker who did nothing much but wink. That old joker, though, he let me off, so I've nothing agen' *him*. He's a white man, he is. So here I am at last, having got your invitation to lunch, ma'am, just half-an-hour ago."

Sir Joseph Todd had been making fruitless efforts to rise, unaided, from his chair; he now caught Claude's arm, and simultaneously, the eye of the Duke.

"Jumping Moses!" roared Jack; "why, there he is! I beg your pardon, mister; but who'd have thought of finding *you* here?"

"This is pleasing," muttered Edmund Stubbs, in the background, to his friend the Impressionist. "I've seen the lion and the lamb lie down here together before to-day. But nothing like this!"

The Impressionist whipped out a pencil and bared a shirt-cuff. No one saw him. All eyes were upon the Duke and the magistrate, who were shaking hands.

"You have paid me a valuable compliment," croaked Sir Joseph gayly. "Of course I winked! Hadn't I my Lord Duke's little peccadillo to wink at?"

And he bowed himself away under cover of

his joke, which also helped Lady Caroline
enormously. The Duke mentioned the name
by which he would go down to posterity on a
metropolitan charge-sheet. Most people resumed their conversation. A few still laughed.
And the less seriously the whole matter was
taken, the better, of course, for all concerned,
particularly the Duke. Olivia had him in
hand now. And her mother found time to
exchange a few words with Claude Lafont.

"A dear fellow, is he not? So natural!
Such an example in that way to us all! How
many of us would carry ourselves as well in —
in our bush garments?" speculated her Ladyship, for the benefit of more ears than Claude's.
Then her voice sank and trembled. "Take him
away, Claude," she gasped below her breath.
"Take him away!"

"I intend to," he whispered, nodding, "when
I get the chance."

"But not only from here — from town as well.
Carry him off to the Towers! And when you
get him there, for heaven's sake keep him
there, and take him in hand, and we will all
come down in August to see what you have
done."

"I'm quite agreeable, of course; but what if
he isn't?"

"He will be. *You* can do what you like with him. I have discovered that already; he asked at once if you were here, and said how he liked you. Claude, you are so clever and so good! If any one can make him presentable, it is you!" She was wringing her white hands whiter yet.

"I'll do my best, for all our sakes. I must say I like my material."

"Oh, he's a dear fellow!" cried Lady Caroline, dropping her hands and uplifting her voice once more. "So original — in nothing more than in his moral courage — his superiority to mere conventional appearances! *That* is a lesson ——"

Lady Caroline stopped with a little scream. In common with others, she had heard the high, shrill mewing of a kitten; but cats were a special aversion of her Ladyship's.

"What was that?" she cried, tugging instinctively at her skirts.

"Meow!" went the shrill small voice again; and all eyes fastened upon the Duke of St. Osmund's, whose ready-made coat-tails were moving like a bag of ferrets.

The Duke burst into a hearty laugh, and diving in his coat-tail pocket, produced the offending kitten in his great fist. Lady Caroline Sellwood took a step backward; and because she did not lead it, there was no laugh this time from her guests; and because there was no laugh but his own, the Duke looked consciously awkward for the first time. In fact, it was the worst moment yet; the next, however, Olivia's pink palms were stretched out for the kitten, and Olivia's laughing voice was making the sweetest music that ever had gladdened the heart of the Duke.

"The little darling!" cried the girl with genuine delight. "Let me have it, do!"

He gave it to her without a word, but with eyes that clung as fast to her face as the tiny claws did to her dress. Olivia's attention was all for the kitten; she was serenely unconscious of that devouring gaze; but Claude saw it, and winced. And Lady Caroline saw it too.

"Poor mite!" pursued Olivia, stroking the bunch of black fur with a cheek as soft. "What a shame to keep it smothered up in a stuffy pocket! Are you fond of cats?" she asked the Duke.

"Am I not! They were my only mates up the bush. I brought over three besides the kitten."

"You brought them from the bush?"

"I did so!"

Olivia looked at him; his eyes had never left her; she dropped hers, and caressed the kitten.

"I put that one in my pocket," continued the Duke, "because I learned Livingstone to ride in front of me when he was just such another little 'un. But he'd done a bolt in the night; I found him just now with his three working paws black with your London soot; but he wasn't there when I got up, so I took the youngster. P'r'aps it wasn't over kind. It won't happen again. He's yours!"

"The kitten?"

"Why, certainly."

"To keep?"

"If you will. I'd be proud!"

"Then *I* am proud. And I'll try to be as kind to it as you would have been."

"You're uncommon kind to me," remarked the Duke irrelevantly. "So are you all," he added, in a ringing voice, as he drew himself up to his last inch, and for once stood clear of the medium height. "I never knew that there were so many of you here, or I'd have kept away. I'm just as I stepped off of the ship. I went aboard pretty much as I left the bush; if you'll make allowances for me this time, it sha'n't happen again. You don't catch me twice in a rig like this! Meanwhile, it's very kind of you all not to laugh at a fellow. I'm much obliged to you. I am so. And I hope we shall know each other better before long!"

Claude was not ashamed of him then. There was no truer dignity beneath the ruffles and periwigs of their ancestors in the Maske picture-gallery than that of the rude, blunt fellow who could face modestly and yet kindly a whole roomful of well-dressed Londoners. It did not desert him as he shook hands with Lady Caroline and Olivia. In another moment the Duke was gone, and of his own accord, before he had been twenty minutes in the house. And what remained of that Wednesday afternoon fell flat and stale — always excepting the little formula with which Lady Caroline Sellwood sped her parting guests.

"Poor fellow," it ran, "he has roughed it so dreadfully in that horrible bush! You won't know him the next time you see him. Yes, I assure you, he went straight on board at that end and came straight to us at this! Not a day for anything in Melbourne or here. Actually not one day! I thought it so dear of him to come as he was. Didn't you?"

CHAPTER V

THE ragged beard had been trimmed to a point; the uncouth hair had been cut, shampooed, and invested with a subtle, inoffensive aroma; and a twenty-five-shilling Lincoln and Bennett crowned all without palpable incongruity. The brown, chapped neck, on the other hand, did look browner and rougher than before in the cold clutch of a gleaming stand-up collar. And a like contrast was observable between the ample cuffs of a brand-new shirt, and the Duke's hands, on whose hirsute backs the yellow freckles now stood out like half-sovereigns. Jack drew the line at gloves. On the whole, however, his docility had passed all praise; he even consented to burden himself with a most superfluous Inverness cape, all for the better concealment of the ready-made suit. In fine. a few hours had made quite a painfully new man of him; yet perhaps the only real loss was that of his good spirits; and these he had left, not in any of the shops to which Claude had taken him before dinner, but, since then, in his own house in Belgrave Square.

Claude had shown him over it between nine and ten; they were now arm-in-arm on their way from this errand, and the street-lamps shone indifferently on the Duke's dejection and on Claude's relief. He had threatened instant occupation of his own town-house; he had conceived nightmare hospitalities towards all and sundry; and had stuck to his guns against argument with an obstinacy which made Claude's hair stand on end. Now the Duke had less to say. He had seen his house. The empty, echoing, inhospitable rooms, with perhaps a handful of electric lights freezing out of the darkness as they entered, had struck a chill to his genial heart. And Claude knew it as he led the way to his own cosy chambers; but was reminded of another thing as he approached them, and became himself, on the spot, a different man.

He had forgotten the two friends he had invited to come in for a private view of the large-paper edition. He was reminded of them by seeing from the street his open window filled with light; and his manner had entirely altered when he detained the Duke below, and sought with elaborate phrases to impress him beforehand with the transcendent merits of the couple whom he was about to meet. Jack promptly offered to go away. He had never heard tell of Impressionism, and artists were not in his line. What about the other joker? What did *he* do?

"Nothing, my dear fellow; he's far too good a man to *do* things," explained Claude, whose changed speech inclined the other to flight quite as much as his accounts of the men upstairs. "The really delicate brains — the most highly sensitised souls — seldom spend themselves upon mere creative work. They look on, and possibly criticise — that is, when they meet with aught worthy their criticism. My friend, Edmund Stubbs, is such an one. He has a sensitised soul, if you like! His artistic standard is too high, he is too true to his ideals, to produce the imperfect. He is full of ideas; but they are too big for brush, pen, or chisel to express them. On the other hand, he's a very fountain of inspiration, tempered by critical restraint, to many a man whose name (as my own) is possibly a household word in Clapham, where poor Edmund's is unknown. Not that I should pity him on that score; he has a holy scorn for what himself would call a 'suburban popularity'; and, indeed, I am not with him in his views as to the indignity of fame generally. But there, he is a bright particular star who is content to shine for

F

the favoured few who have the privilege of calling him their friend."

"You do talk like a book, and no error!" said
the Duke. "I haven't ever heard you gas on
like that before."

The bright particular star was discovered in
Claude's easiest chair, with the precious volume
in one hand, and a tall glass, nearly empty, in
the other; the Impressionist was in the act of
replacing the stopper in the whisky-decanter;
and Claude accepted the somewhat redundant
explanation, that they were making themselves
at home, with every sign of approval. Nor was
he slow in introducing his friends; but for once
the Duke was refreshingly subdued, if not shy;
and for the first few minutes the others had their
heads together over the large-paper edition, for
whose "decorations" the draftsman himself had
not the least to say, where all admired. At
length Claude passed the open volume to his
cousin; needless to say it was open at the fron-
tispiece; but the first and only thing that Jack
saw was the author's name in red capitals on the
title-page opposite.

"Claude Lafont!" he read out. "Why, you
don't ever mean — to tell me — that's you, old
brusher?"

Claude smiled and coloured.

"You an author!" continued the Duke in a wide-eyed wonder. "And you never told me! Well, no wonder you can talk like a book when you can write one, too! So this is your latest, is it?"

"The limited large-paper edition," said Claude. "Only seventy-five copies printed, and I sign them all. How does it strike you — physically, I mean?"

"'Physically' is quite pleasing," murmured Stubbs; and Claude helped him to more whisky.

Jack looked at the book. The back was of a pale brown cardboard; the type had a curious, olden air about it; the paper was thick, and its edges elaborately ragged. The Duke asked if it was a new book. It looked to him a hundred years old, he said, and discovered that he had paid a pretty compliment unawares.

"There's one thing, however," he added: "we could chop leaves as well as that in the back-blocks!"

The Impressionist grinned; his friend drank deep, with a corrugated brow; the poet expounded the beauties of the rough edge, and Jack gave him back his book.

"I know nothing about it," said he; "but still, I'm proud of you, I am so. And I'm proud," he added, "to find myself in such company as yours, gentlemen; though I don't mind telling you, if I'd known I'd be the only plain man in the room I'd never have come upstairs!"

And the Duke sat down in a corner, with his knife, his tobacco, and his cutty-pipe, as shy as a great boy in a roomful of girls. Yet this wore off, for the conversation of the elect did not, after all, rarefy the atmosphere to oppression; indeed, that of the sensitised soul contained more oaths than Jack had heard from one mouth since he left the bush, and this alone was enough to put him at his ease. At the same time he was repelled, for it appeared to be a characteristic of the great Stubbs to turn up his nose at all men; and as that organ was *retroussé* to begin with, Jack was forcibly reminded of some ill-bred, snarling bulldog, and he marvelled at the hound's reputation. He put in no word, however, until the conversation turned on Claude's poems, and a particularly cool, coarse thing was said of one of them, and Claude only laughed. Then he did speak up.

"See here, mister," he blurted out from his corner. "Could you do as good?"

Stubbs stared at the Duke, and drained his glass.

"I shouldn't try," was his reply.

"I wouldn't," retorted Jack. "I just wouldn't, if I were you."

Stubbs could better have parried a less indelicate, a less childish thrust; as it was, he reached for his hat. Claude interfered at once.

"My dear old fellow," said he to Jack, "you mustn't mind what my friend Edmund says of my stuff. I like it. He is always right, for one thing; and then, only think of the privilege of having such a critic to tell one exactly what he thinks."

Jack looked from one man to the other. The sincerity of the last speech was not absolutely convincing, but that of Claude's feeling for his friend was obvious enough; and, with a laugh, the Duke put his back against the door. The apology which he delivered in that position was in all respects characteristic. It was unnecessarily full; it was informed alike by an extravagant good-will towards mankind, and an irritating personal humility; and it ended, somewhat to Claude's dismay, with a direct invitation to both his friends to spend a month at Maske Towers.

Perhaps these young men realised then, for the first time, who the rough fellow was, after all, with whom they had been thrown in contact. At all events the double invitation was accepted with alacrity; and no more hard things were said of Claude's lyrics. The flow of soul was henceforth as uninterrupted as that of the whisky down the visitors' throats. And no further hitch would have occurred had the Impressionist not made that surreptitious sketch of the Duke, which so delighted his friends.

"Oh, admirable!" cried Claude. "A most suggestive humouresque!"

"It'll do," said Stubbs, the oracle. "It mightn't appeal to the suburbs, damn them, but it does to us."

"Grant the convention, and the art is perfect," continued Claude, with the tail of his eye on Jack.

"It is the caricature that is more like than life," pursued Stubbs, with a sidelong glance in the same direction.

Jack saw these looks; but from his corner he could not see the sketch, nor had he any suspicion of its subject. All else that he noted was the flush of triumph, or it may have been whisky, or just possibly both, on the pale, fringed face of Impressionism. He held out his hand for the half-sheet of paper on which the sketch had been made.

"I hope it won't offend you," exclaimed the artist, hesitating.

"Offend me! Why should it? Let's have a look!"

And he looked for more than a minute at the five curves and a beard which had expressed to quicker eyes the quintessence of his own outward and visible personality. At first he could make nothing of them; even when an interpretation dawned upon him, his face was puzzled as he raised it to the trio hanging on his words.

"It 'won't do, mister," said the Duke reluctantly. "You'll never get saplings like them," tapping the five curves with his forefinger, "to hold a nest like that," putting his thumb on the beard, "and don't you believe it."

There was a moment's silence. Then the Impressionist said thickly:

"Give me that sketch."

Jack handed it back. In another moment it was littering the ground in four pieces, and the door had banged behind the indignant draftsman.

"What on earth have I done?" cried the Duke, aghast.

"You have offended Llewellyn," replied Claude shortly.

"How? By what I said? I'll run after him this minute and apologise. I never meant to hurt his feelings. Where's that stove-pipe hat?"

"Let *me* go," said Stubbs, getting up. "I

understand the creative animal; it is thin-skinned; but I'll tell our friend what you say."

"I wish you would. Tell him I meant no harm. And fetch him down with you just whenever you can come."

"Thanks — that will be very pleasing. I daresay August will be our best time, but we shall let you know. I'll put it all right with Ivor; but these creative asses (saving your presence, Lafont) never can see a joke."

"A joke!" cried Jack, when he and Claude were alone.

"Stubbs is ironical," said Claude severely.

"Look here," said the Duke, "what are you givin' us, old boy? Seems to me you clever touchers have been getting at a cove between you. Where does this joke come in, eh?"

And his good faith was so obvious that Claude picked up the four quarters of torn paper, fitted them together, and entered upon yet another explanation. This one, however, was somewhat impatiently given and received. The Duke professed to think his likeness exceedingly unlike — when, indeed, he could be got to see his own outlines at all — and Claude disagreeing, a silence fell between the pair. Jack sought to break it by taking off his collar (which had made him miserable) and putting it in his pocket with a significant look; but the act provoked no comment. So the two men sat, the one smoking cigarettes, the other his cutty, but neither speaking, nor yet reading a line. And the endless roar of Piccadilly, reaching them through the open windows, emphasised their silence, until suddenly it sank beneath the midnight chimes of the city clocks. In another minute a tiny, tinkling echo came from Claude's chimney-piece, and the Duke put down his pipe and spoke.

"My first whole day in London—a goner," he said; "and a pretty full day it's been. Listen to this for one day's work," and as he rehearsed them, he ticked off the events on his great brown fingers. "Got run in—that's number one. Turned up among a lot of swells in my old duds—number two. Riled the cleverest man you know—number three—so that he nearly cleared out of your rooms; and, not content with that, hurt the feelings of the second cleverest (present company excepted) so that he *did* clear—which is number four. Worst of all, riled you, old man, and hurt your feelings too. That's the finisher. And see here, Claude, it isn't good enough and it won't do. I won't wash in London, and I'm full up

of the hole; as for my own house, it gave me
the fair hump the moment I put my nose inside; and I'd be on to make tracks up the
bush any day you like — if it weren't for one
thing."

" What's that," said Claude, "if it's a fair
question?"

The other concealed his heightened colour
by relighting his pipe and puffing vigorously.

" I'll tell you," said he; "it's that old girl
and — what's the daughter's name again?"

" Olivia."

" Olivia.   A beautiful name for a beautiful
girl!   She's all that and more."

" And much more."

" You see, she's as good inside as out; she
has a kind heart."

" I have always found it so," said Claude,
"and I've known her since she was a child."

The two kinsmen, who had been so wide
apart a few minutes since, were now more than
ever mutually akin. They drew their chairs
together; but the touchstone was deep down
in either heart.

" You knew her when she was a child!" repeated the Duke in a kind of awe. "Yes; and
I daresay, now, you used to play with her, and
perhaps take her on your knee, and even pull

her hair and kiss her in them old days. Yet there you sit smoking cigarettes!"

His own pipe was out. He was in a reverie. Claude also had his own thoughts.

"The one thing was this," said the Duke at length: "would the old woman and her daughter come to see us up the country?"

Claude was torn two ways. The Towers scheme was no longer his first anxiety. He returned to it by an effort.

"They would," he said. "Lady Caroline told me so. They would come like a shot in August. She said so herself."

"Would you put me up to things in the meantime? Would you be showing me the ropes?"

"The very thing I should like to do, so far as I am able."

"Then we'll start to-morrow — I mean to-day. That settles it. And yet —— "

"Out with it," said Claude, smiling.

"Well, I will. I mean no harm,.you understand. Who am I to dare to look at her? Only I do feel as if that girl would do me a deal of good down there — you know, in making me more the sort of chap for my billet. But if she's gone and got a sweetheart, he might very easily object; so I just thought I'd like to know."

"She hasn't one, to my knowledge," said Claude at length.

"Is that a fact?" cried the Duke. "Well, I don't know what all you fellows are thinking of, but I do know that I am jolly glad. Not from any designs of my own, mind you — I haven't as much cheek as all that — but to save trouble. Do you know, Claudy, I've had a beast of a thought off and on all the night?"

"No; what was that?"

"Why, I half suspected she was your own girl."

CHAPTER VI

A NEW LEAF

"The Duke of St. Osmund's and Mr. Claude Lafont left town yesterday for Maske Towers, the family seat near Devenholme." So ran the announcement in the morning papers of the next day but one. And the Duke was actually exploring his inheritance when it appeared.

Overnight the pair had arrived too late to see much more than the lofty, antique hall and the respective rooms in which they were to sup and sleep; but the birds awoke Jack in the early morning, and he was up and out before seven o'clock.

As yet he had seen little that attracted him within, and at this hour he felt a childish horror of the dark colossal canvases overhanging the grand staircase and the hall; like the sightless suits of armour standing blind sentinel below, they froze him with the look of lifeless life about the grim, gigantic figures. He was thankful to see one of the great double doors standing open to the sun; it let him out into a portico loftier than the hall; and folding his arms across a stone balustrade, the whilom bushman looked forth between Corinthian columns like the masts of a ship, and was monarch of all he beheld.

A broad and stately terrace ran right and left below; beyond and below this, acres of the smoothest, greenest sward were relieved by a few fine elms, with the deer still in clusters about their trunks. The lawn sloped quietly to the verdant shores of a noble lake; sun and dew had dusted the grass with silver; sun and wind were rippling the lake with flakes of flame like leaping gold-fish; and across the water, on the rising ground, a plantation of young pines ran their points into the radiant sky. These trees appealed to the Duke more than anything he had seen yet. His last bush hut had been built among pines; and such is the sentimental attraction of the human heart towards a former condition — better or worse, if it be but beyond recall — that the Duke of St. Osmund's had to inspect that plantation before anything else. Leaving the Towers behind him, unnoticed and indeed forgotten, he crossed the lawn, skirted the lake, and plunged amid the pine-trees as his impulse spurred him. But on his way back, a little later, the mellow grandeur of

that ancient pile broke in upon him at last, and
he stood astounded in the wet grass, the blood
of possession running hot in his veins.

The historic building stretched on this side
for something like a quarter of a mile from end
to end. Here the blue sky sank deep between
turret and spire, and there it picked out a line
of crumbling battlements, or backed the upper
branches of an elm that (from this point) cut
the expanse of stone in two. It had grown out
of many attempts in as many ages ; thus, besides
architectural discrepancies for the eyes of the
few, the shading of the walls was as finely
graduated as that of an aging beard, but the
prevailing tint was a pearly gray, now washed
with purple, and exquisitely softened by the
tender haze still lingering in the dewy air. And
from every window that Jack could see, flashed
a morning sun ; for as he stood and looked, his
shadow lay in front of him along the milky
grass.

To one extremity of the building clung an
enormous conservatory, likewise ablaze from
dome to masonry ; at the other, the dark hues
of a shrubbery rested the eye ; but that of the
Duke was used to the sunlit desert, and not
readily dazzled. His quick glance went like a
bullet through the trees to a red gable and the

gilt hands of a clock just visible beyond. On the instant he recovered from his enchantment, and set off for the shrubbery at a brisk walk; for he had heard much of the Maske stables, and evidently there they were.

As he was in the shrubbery, the stable clock struck eight after a melodious chime sadly spoilt by the incessant barking of some small dog; the last stroke reverberated as he emerged, and the dog had the morning air to itself, to murder with its hideous clamour. But the Duke now saw the exciting cause, and it excited *him;* for he had come out opposite the stable-yard gates, which were shut, but from the top of which, with its lame paw lifted, a vertical tail, and a back like a hedgehog asleep, his own yellow cat spat defiance at an unseen foe. And between the barks came the voice of a man inciting the dog with a filthy relish.

"Set him off, Pickle! Now's your time. Try again. Oh, blow me, if you can't you can't, and I'll have to lend you a hand."

And one showed over the gate with the word, but the fingers grabbed the air, for Jack had snatched his pet in the nick of time. He was now busy with the ring of the latch, fumbling it in his fury. The breath came in gusts through his set teeth and bristling beard. One hand clasped the yellow cat in a fierce caress; the other knotted into a fist as the gate flew open.

In the yard a hulking, smooth-faced fellow, whose pendulous under-lip had dropped in dismay, changed his stare for a grin when he saw the Duke, who was the smaller as well as the rougher-looking man of the two; for he had not only come out without his collar, which he discarded whenever he could; but he had clapped on the old bush wideawake because Claude was not up to stop him.

"Well, and who are you?" began the other cheerfully.

"You take off your coat and I'll show you," replied Jack, with a blood-thirsty indistinctness. "I'm a better man than you are, whoever I am; at least we'll have a see!"

"Oh, will we?" said the fellow. "And you're the better man, are you? What do *you* think?" he added, turning to a stable-boy who stood handy with thin brown arms akimbo, and thumbs in his belt.

"I wonder 'oo 'e thinks 'e is w'en 'e's at 'ome?" said the lad.

Jack never heard him. He had spied the saddle-room door standing open. In an instant he was there, with the small dog yelping at his heels; in another, he had locked the door between cat and dog, pocketed the key, and returned to his man, stripping off his own coat and waistcoat as he came. He flung them into a corner, and after them his bush hat.

"Now let's see you take off yours! If you don't," added Jack, with a big bush oath, "I'll have to hide you with it on!"

But man and boy had been consulting while his back was turned, and Jack now found himself between the two of them; not that he gave the lad a thought.

"Look you here; I'll tell you who *I* am," said the man. "My name's Matt Hunt, and Matt can fight, as you wouldn't need telling if you belonged to these parts. But he don't take on stray tramps like you; so, unless you hook it slippy, we're just going to run you out o' this yard quicker than you come in."

"Not till I've shown you how to treat dumb animals ——"

"Then here goes!"

And with that the man Hunt seized one of Jack's arms, while the stable-boy nipped the other from behind, and made a dive at Jack's pocket for the saddle-room key. But a flat-footed kick sent the lad sprawling without harming him; and the man was driven so hard under the nose that he too fell back, bearded with blood.

“Come on!” roared Jack. “And you, my boy, keep out of the light unless you want a whipping yourself!”

He was rolling up the sleeves from his tanned and furry arms. Hunt followed suit, a cascade of curses flowing with his blood; he had torn off his coat, and a wrist-button tinkled on the cement as he caught up Jack in his preparations. His arms were thicker than the bushman’s, though white and fleshy. Hunt was also the heavier weight, besides standing fully six feet, as against the Duke’s five-feet-nine when he held himself up. Nor was there any lack of confidence in the dripping, hairless, sinister face, when the two men finally squared up.

They fell to work without niggling, for Jack rushed in like a bull, leading most violently with his left. It was an inartistic start; the big man was not touched; but neither did he touch Jack, who displayed, at all events, a quick pair of legs. Yet it was this start that steadied the Duke. It showed him that Hunt was by no means unskilled in the use of his hands; and it put out of his head everything but the fight itself, so that he heard no more the small tike barking outside the saddle-room door, hitherto his angriest goad.

Some cool sparring ensued. Then Hunt let out from the shoulder, but the blow was avoided with great agility; then Jack led off again, but with a lighter touch, and this time he drew his man. The blows of the next minute it was impossible to follow. They were given and returned with enormous virulence. And there was no end to them until the big man tripped and fell.

"See here," said Jack, standing over him; "that was my cat, and I'd got to go for you. But if you've had enough of this game, so have I, and we'll cry quits."

He was sucking a cut lip as he spoke. The other spat out a tooth and blundered to his feet.

"Quits, you scum? Wait a bit!"

And they were at hotter work than ever.

Meanwhile the yard was filling with stablemen and gardeners, who were in time to see Hunt striding down on his unknown adversary, and the latter retreating in good order; but the stride quickened, ending in a rush, which the Duke eluded so successfully that he was able to hit Hunt hard on the ear as he passed.

It was afterwards a relief to the spectators to remember how they had applauded this effort. To the Duke their sympathy was a comfort at the time; though he no more suspected that his adversary was also his most unpopular tenant, than the latter dreamt of his being the Duke.

Hunt let out a bellow of pain, staggered, and resumed his infuriate rush; but his punishment was now heavier than before. He had lost both wind and head, and he was losing pluck. One of his eyes was already retiring behind folds of livid flesh; and a final blow under the nose, where the first of all had been delivered, knocked him howling into the arms of a new-comer, who disengaged himself as Hunt fell.

"What, Claude, is that you?" cried the Duke; and a flood of new sensations so changed his voice, that Hunt looked up from where he lay, a beaten, bleeding, blubbering mass. But in the silent revelation of that moment there was at first no sound save the barking of the fox-terrier outside the saddle-room door. This had never ceased. Then the coachman's pipe fell from his mouth and was smashed.

"My God!" said he. "It's his Grace himself!"

He had driven the Duke from Devenholme the night before.

"The Duke of St. Osmund's!" exclaimed Hunt from the ground. He had been shedding blood and tears indifferently, and now he sat up with a slimy stare in his uninjured eye.

"Yes, that's right," said Jack, with a nod to the company. "So now you all know what to expect for cruelty to cats, or any other dumb animals; and don't you forget it!"

He put on his coat and went over to the saddle-room. Claude followed him, still at a loss for words. And Hunt's dog went into a wild ecstasy as the key was put into the lock.

"Hold him," said Jack. "The dog's all right; and I lay his master 'll think twice before he sets him on another cat o' mine."

"Come away," said Claude hoarsely; "for all our sakes, come away before you make bad worse!"

"Well, I will. Only hold him tight. That's it. Poor little puss, then — poor old Livingstone! Now I'm ready; come along."

But Hunt was in their path; and Jack's heart smote him for the mischief he had done, though his own lower lip was swollen like a sausage.

"So you're the new Duke of St. Osmund's," said Hunt, with a singular deliberation. "I wasn't to know that, of course; no, by gosh, not likely!"

"Well, you know it now," was the reply. "And — and I'm sorry I had to hit you so hard, Hunt!"

"Oh, don't apologise," said Hunt, with a sneer that showed a front tooth missing. "Stop a bit, though; I'm not so sure," he added, with a glance of evil insight.

"Sure of what?"

"Whether you oughtn't to apologise for not hitting a man of your own age!"

"Take no notice of him," whispered Claude strenuously; but he obtained none himself.

"Nonsense," said the Duke; "you're the younger man, at all events."

"Am I? I was born in '59, *I* was."

"Then according to all accounts you're the younger man by four years."

"By — four — years," repeated Hunt slowly. "So you was born in '55! Thank you; I shall make a note of that, you may be sure — your Grace!"

And Hunt was gone; they heard him whistling for his tike when he was himself out of sight, and the dog went at last. Then the coachman stepped forward, cap in hand.

"If you please, your Grace, that man was here without my knowledge. He's always putting in his nose where he isn't wanted; I've shifted him out of this before to-day; and with your Grace's permission, I'll give orders not to have him admitted again."

"Who is he?" said Jack.   "A tenant or what?"

"Only a tenant, your Grace. Matt Hunt, they call him, of the Lower Farm; but it might be of Maske Towers, by the way he goes on!"

"He took a mighty interest in my age," remarked the Duke. "I never asked to look at *his* fangs — but I think you'll find one of them somewhere about the yard. No; I'm not fond of fighting, my lads. Don't you run away with that idea. But there's one thing I can't and won't suffer, and that's cruelty to animals. You chaps in the stables recollect that! And so good-morning to you all."

Claude led the way through the shrubbery in a deep depression. The guilty Duke took his arm with one hand, while with the other he hugged the yellow cat that was eying the shrubbery birds over its master's shoulder, much as the terrier had eyed it.

"My dear old boy," said Jack, "I'm as sorry as sorry for what's happened. But I couldn't help myself. Look at Livingstone; he'd have been a stiff 'un by this time if I hadn't turned up when I did; so naturally there was a row. Still I'm sorry. I know it's a bad beginning; and I remember saying in the train that I'd turn over a new leaf down here. Well, and so I will if you give me time. Don't judge me by this morning, Claude. Give me another chance; and for God's sake don't look like that!"

"I can't help it, Jack," replied Claude, with a weary candour. "I'm prepared for anything now. You make me a year older every day. How do I know what you'll do next? I think the best thing I can do is to give you up as a bad job."

CHAPTER VII

THE DUKE'S PROGRESS

CLAUDE'S somewhat premature despair was not justified by the event; nevertheless it did good. Excusable enough at the time, that little human outbreak was also more effective than the longest lecture or the most mellifluous reproof. Jack liked his cousin. The liking was by no means unconnected with gratitude. And now Jack saw that he could best show his gratitude by adopting a more suitable course of conduct than he could claim to have pursued hitherto. He determined to make an effort. He had everything to learn; it was a mountainous task that lay before him; but he faced it with spirit, and made considerable progress in a little space.

He learnt how to treat the servants. The footmen had misbehaved when he addressed them as "my boy" and "old toucher" from his place at table. He consulted Claude, and dropped these familiarities as well as the pain-

fully respectful tone which he had at first
employed towards old Stebbings, the butler.
Stebbings had been very many years in the
family. The deference inspired by his vener-
able presence was natural enough in the new
Duke of St. Osmund's; but it shocked and dis-
tressed Stebbings's feudal soul. He complained
to Claude, and he had not to complain twice.
For Jack discovered a special and a touching
eagerness to master the rudiments of etiquette:
though in other respects (which certainly mattered less) he was still incorrigible.

His social "crammer" could no more cure
him of his hatred of a collar than of his liking
for his cats. The latter were always with him;
the former, unhappily, was not. In these things
the Duke was hopelessly unregenerate; he was
a stockman still at heart, and a stockman he
threatened to remain. The soft summer nights
were nothing to the nights in the bush; the
fleecy English sky was not blue at all after the
skies of Riverina; and the Duke's ideal of a
man was "my old boss." Claude heard of "my
old boss" until he was sick of the words, which
constituted a gratuitous reminder of a position
most men would have been glad to forget. Yet
there was much to be thankful for. There were
no more scenes such as the Duke's set-to in

his own stable-yard with one of his own tenants. At least nothing of the sort happened again until Jack's next collision with Matthew Hunt. And that was not yet.

Matthew was from home when the Duke, making a round of the estate, with his agent, visited the Lower Farm in its turn. Old Hunt, Matthew's besotted father, received them in the kitchen with a bloodshot stare and little else, for drink had long dimmed his forces. Not so the old man's daughter-in-law, Matthew's wife, who showed the visitors all over the farm in a noiseless manner that made Jack feel uneasy, because he never knew when she was or was not at his elbow. Besides, he could not forget the thrashing he had given her husband, nor yet suppose that she had forgotten it either. The woman was of a gross type strangely accentuated by her feline quietude. She had a continual smile, and sly eyes that dropped when they encountered those of the Duke, whom they followed sedulously at all other moments. Jack seemed to know it, too; at all events he was not sorry to turn his back upon the Lower Farm.

"A rum lot, the Hunts!" he said at lunch. "They're about the only folks here that I haven't cottoned to on the spot. I shall get on fine with all the others. But I can't suffer those Hunts!"

"There's no reason why you should suffer them," observed the agent, in his well-bred drawl; for he had a more aristocratic manner than Claude himself. "They have the best farm on the property, and they pay the smallest rent. You should think over my suggestion of this morning."

"No, no," said the Duke. "He wants me to double the rent, Claude, and clear them out if they won't pay. I can't do it."

"Well, no; I hardly think you can," assented Claude. "Oddly enough, my grandfather had quite a weakness for the Hunts; and then they are very old tenants. That hoary-headed Silenus, whom you saw, was once in the stables here; so was his son after him, in my time; and the old man's sister was my grandmother's maid. You can't turn out people like that *ex itinere*, so to speak — I mean to say in a hurry. It's too old a connection altogether."

"Exactly what they trade upon," said the agent. "They have been spoilt for years, and they expect his Grace to go on spoiling them. I should certainly get rid of the whole gang."

"No, mister — no!" declared the Duke. "Claude is right. I can't do it. I might if

I hadn't given that fellow a hiding. After that I simply can't; it would look too bad."

The agent said no more, but his look and shrug were perhaps neither politic nor polite. A strapping sportsman himself, and a person of some polish into the bargain, he was in a position, as it were, to look down on Claude with one eye, and on the Duke with the other. And he did so with a freedom extraordinary in one of his wisdom and understanding.

"One of these days," said Jack, "I shall give that joker his cheque. He's not my notion of an overseer at all; if he's too good for the billet let him roll up his swag and clear out; if he isn't, let him treat the bosses as a blooming overseer should."

"Why, what's the head and chief of his offending now?" asked Claude; for this was one night in the billiard-room, when the agent had been making an example of both cousins at pyramids; it was after he was gone, and while the Duke was still tearing off his collar.

"What has he said to-night?" continued the poet, less poetically. "I heard nothing offensive."

"You wouldn't," said the Duke; "you're such a good sort yourself. You'd never see when a chap was pulling your leg, but I see fast enough, and I won't have it. What did he say to-night? He talked through his neck when we missed our shots. That about billiards in the bush I didn't mind; me and the bush, we're fair game; but when he got on to your poetry, old man, I felt inclined to run my cue through his gizzard. 'A poet's shot,' he says, when you put yourself down; and 'you should write a sonnet about that,' when you got them three balls in together. I don't say it wasn't a fluke. That has nothing at all to do with it. The way the fellow spoke is what I weaken on. He wouldn't have done for my old boss, and I'm blowed if he'll do for me. One of these days I shall tell him to come outside and take his coat off; and, by the looks of him, I shouldn't be a bit surprised to see him put me through."

Claude's anxiety overcame every other feeling. He implored the Duke not to make another scene, least of all with such a man as the agent, whose chaff, he truly protested, did not offend him in the least. Jack shook his head, and was next accused of being more sensitive about the "wretched poems" than was the poet himself. This could not have been. But Claude was not so very far wrong.

His slender book was being widely reviewed, or rather "noticed," for the two things are not quite the same. The "notices," on the whole, were good and kind, but "uninstructed," so Claude said with a sigh; nevertheless, he appeared to obtain a sneaking satisfaction from their perusal; and as for Jack, he would read them aloud, capering round the room and shaking Claude by both hands in his delighted enthusiasm. To him every printed compliment was a loud note blown from the trumpet of fame into the ears of all the world. He would hear not a word against the paper in which it appeared, but attributed every qualifying remark of Claude's to the latter's modesty, and each favourable paragraph to some great responsible critic voicing the feeling of the country in the matter of these poems. Claude himself, however, though frequently gratified, was not deceived; for the sweetest nothings came invariably from the provincial press; and he at least knew too much to mistake a "notice" for a "real review."

The real reviews were a sadly different matter. There were very few of them, in the first place; their scarcity was worse than their severity. And they were generally very severe indeed; or they did not take the book seriously, which, as Claude said, was the unkindest cut of all.

"Only show me the skunk who wrote that,"

exclaimed Jack one morning, looking over Claude's shoulder as he opened his press-cuttings, "and I'll give him the biggest hiding ever he had in his life!"

Another critic, the writer of a really sympathetic and exhaustive review, the Duke desired to invite to Maske Towers by the next post, "because," said Jack, "he must be a real good sort, and we ought to know him."

"I do know him," said Claude, with a groan, for he had thought of keeping the fact to himself; "I know him to my cost. He owes me money. This is payment on account. Oh, I am no good! I must give it up! Ignorance and interest alone are at my back! Genuine enthusiasm there is none!"

There was Jack's. But was that genuine? The Duke himself was not sure. He meant it to ring true, but then he meant to appreciate the poems, and of many of them he could make little enough in his secret soul.

All this, however, was but one side of the quiet life led by the cousins at Maske Towers; and it had but one important effect — that of sowing in Claude's heart a loyalty to Jack not unworthy of Jack's loyalty to him.

There were other subjects of discussion upon which the pair were by no means at one. There was Jack's open failure to appreciate the marble halls, the resonant galleries, the darkling pictures of his princely home; and there was the scatter-brained scheme by which he ultimately sought to counteract the oppressive grandeur of his new surroundings.

It was extremely irritating, especially to a man like Claude; but the proudest possessions of their ancestors (whose superlative taste and inferior morals had been the byword of so many ages) were those which appealed least to that blameless Goth, the ninth Duke of St. Osmund's. The most glaring case in point was that of the pictures, which alone would make the world-wide fame of a less essentially noble seat than Maske Towers. But Titian, Rembrandt, Rubens, Leonardo da Vinci, Andrea del Sarto, Angeletti Vernet, and Claude Lorrain—all these were mere names, and new ones, to Happy Jack. Claude Lafont, pointing to magnificent examples of the work of one Old Master after another, made his observations with bated breath, as well he might, for where is there such another private collection? Jack, however, was not impressed; he was merely amazed at Claude, and his remarks in the picture-gallery are entirely unworthy of reproduction. In the State Apartments he was still more trying. He spoke of having the ancient tapestries (after Raphael's Cartoons) taken out and "well shaken," which, as Claude said, would have reduced them to immediate atoms. And he threatened to have the painted ceilings whitewashed without delay.

"Aurora Banishing Night, eh?" he cried, with horizontal beard and upturned eyes. "She'd jolly soon banish *my* night, certainly; it should be,-banishing sleep! And all those naked little nippers! They ought to be papered over, for decency's sake; and that brute of a bed, who would sleep in it, I should like to know? Not me. Not much! It must be twenty-foot high and ten-foot wide; it gives me the hump to look at it, and the ceilings give it me worse. See here, Claude, we'll lock up these State Apartments, as you call them, and you shall keep the key. I'm full of 'em; they'll give me bad dreams as it is."

They were not, however, the only apartments of which the Duke disapproved; the suite which had been done up entirely for his own use, under Claude's direction, did not long commend itself to the ex-stockman. Everything was far too good for him and his cats; they were not accustomed to such splendour; it made them all four uncomfortable — so Jack declared after taking Claude's breath away with the eccentric

plan on which he had set his heart. And for
the remainder of their solitary companionship
each man had his own occupation; the Duke
preparing more congenial quarters for himself
and the cats; and Claude, with Jack's permission and the agent's skilled advice, superintend-
ing the making of private golf-links for Mr.
Sellwood's peculiar behoof. For the Home Secretary had promised to join the Maske party, for
the week-ends at any rate, until (as he expressed
it) the Government " holed out."

That party was now finally arranged. The
Frekes were coming with the Sellwoods, and
the latter family were to have the luxurious
suite which the Duke himself disdained. This
was his Grace's own idea. Moreover, he interested himself personally in the right ordering
of the rooms during the last few days; but
this he kept to himself until the eleventh hour;
in fact, until he was waiting for the drag to
come round, which he was himself going to tool
over to Devenholme to meet his guests. It was
then that certain unexpected misgivings led
Jack to seek out his cousin, in order to take
him to see what he had done.

For Claude had shown him what *he* was doing.
He was producing a set of exceedingly harmless
verses, " To Olivia released from Mayfair," of

which the Duke had already heard the rough draft. The fair copy was in the making even now; in the comparatively small room, at one end of the library, that Jack had already christened the Poet's Corner.

Claude wiped his pen with characteristic care, and then rose readily enough. He followed Jack down the immensely long, galleried, book-lined library, through a cross-fire of coloured lights from the stained-glass windows, and so to the stairs. Overhead there was another long walk, through corridor after corridor, which had always reminded Jack of the hotel in town. But at last, in the newly decorated wing, the Duke took a key from his pocket and put it in a certain door. And now it was Claude who was reminded of the hotel; for a most striking atmospheric change greeted him on the threshold; only this time it was not a gust of heat, but the united perfume of many flowers, that came from within.

The room was fairly flooded with fresh roses. It was as though they had either blown through the open window, or fallen in a miraculous shower from the dainty blue ceiling. They pranked the floor in a fine disorder. They studded the table in tiny vases. They hid the mantelpiece, embedded in moss; from the very grate below, they peeped like fairy flames, breathing fragrance instead of warmth; and some in falling seemed to have caught in the pictures on the walls, so artfully had they been arranged. Only the white narrow bed had escaped the shower. And in the midst of this, his handiwork, stood the Duke, and blushed like the roses themselves.

"Whose room is this?" asked Claude, though he knew so well.

"Olivia's — I should say Miss Sellwood's. You see, old man, you were writing these awfully clever verses for her; so I felt I should like to have something ready too."

"Your poem is the best!" exclaimed Claude, with envious, sparkling eyes. And then he sighed.

"Oh, rot!" said Jack, who was only too thankful for his offering to receive the *cachet* of Claude's approval. "All I wanted was to keep my end up, too. Look here. What do you think of this?"

And he took from a vase on the dressing-table an enormous white bouquet, that opened Claude's eyes wider than before.

"This is for her, too; I wanted to consult you about it," pursued Jack. "Should I leave it here for her, or should I take it down to the station and present it to her there? Or at dinner to-night? I want to know just what you think."

"No, not at dinner," replied Claude; "nor yet at the station."

"Not at all, you mean! I see it in your face!" cried the Duke so that Claude could not answer him. "But why not?" he added vehemently. "Where does the harm come in? It's only a blooming nosegay. What's wrong with it?"

"Nothing," was the reply, "only it might embarrass Olivia."

"Make her uncomfortable?"

"Well, yes; it would be rather marked, you know. A bouquet like that is only fit for a bride."

"I don't see it," said Jack, much crestfallen; "still, if that's so, it's just as well to know it. There was no harm meant. I wasn't thinking of any rot of that kind. However, we don't want to make her uncomfortable; that wasn't the idea at all; so the bouquet's off — like me. Come and let me tool you as far as the boundary fence. I want to show you how we drive four horses up the bush."

The exhibition made Claude a little nervous; there was too much shouting at the horses for his taste, and too much cracking of the whip. Jack could crack a whip better than any man in his own stables. But he accepted Claude's criticism with his usual docility, and dropped him at the gates with his unfailing nod of pure good-humour.

There he sat on the box, in loose rough tweeds of a decent cut, and with the early August sun striking under the brim of a perfectly respectable straw hat, but adding little to the broad light of his own honest, beaming countenance. He waved his whip, and Claude his hand. Then the whip cracked — but only once — and the poet strolled back to his verses, steeped in thought. He had done his best. His soul divined vaguely what the result might mean to him. But his actual thoughts were characteristically permissible; he was merely wondering what Lady Caroline and Olivia Sellwood would say now.

CHAPTER VIII

THE OLD ADAM

OLIVIA said least. Her mother took Claude
by the hand, and thanked him with real tears
in her eyes, for after all she was an Irishwoman,
who could be as emotional as possible when she
chose. As for Mr. Sellwood, he expressed himself as delightfully disappointed in the peer of
whom he had heard so much. Jack struck him
as being an excellent fellow, although not a
golfer, which was a pity, and even apparently
disinclined to take up the game — which might
signify some recondite flaw in his character.
So said the Home Secretary. But Olivia merely
asked who had put all those roses in her room;
and when Claude told her, she simply nodded
and took hardly any notice of the Duke that
night. Yet she wore a handful of his flowers
at her shapely waist. And she did thank him,
in a way.

It was not the sweetest way in the world, as
all her ways had been, these many weeks, in

Jack's imagination. He was grieved and disappointed, but still more was he ashamed. He had taken a liberty. He had alienated his friend. Thus he blamed himself, with bitter, wordless thoughts, and would then fall back upon his disappointment. His feelings were a little mixed. One moment she was not all that he had thought her; the next, she was more than all. She was more beautiful. Often he had tried to recall her face, and tried in vain, having seen her but once before, and then only for a few minutes. Now he perceived that his first impression, blurred and yet dear to him as it had been, had done but meagre justice to Olivia. He had forgotten the delicate dark eyebrows, so much darker than the hair. The girl's radiant colouring had also escaped him. It was like the first faint flush of an Australian dawn. Yet he had missed it in June, just as he had missed the liquid hazel of her eyes; their absolute honesty was what he remembered best; and, by a curious irony, that frank, fine look was the very one which she denied him now.

And so it was from the Friday evening, when the Sellwoods arrived, to the Monday morning when duty recalled the Home Secretary to St. Stephen's. He obeyed the call in no statesman-like frame of mind. He had spent the Sabbath in open sin upon the new-made links, and had been fitly punished by his own execrable play. The athletic agent had made an example of him; he felt that he might just as well have been in church (or rather in the private chapel attached to the Towers), reading the lessons for his son-in-law, Francis Freke; and in the Saturday's "foursome," with the reverend gentleman on his side, the Cabinet Minister had done little better. So he had departed very sorely against the grain, his white hairs bristling with discontent, a broken "driver" hidden away in the depths of his portmanteau. And Olivia, seeing the last of him from amid the tall columns of the portico, felt heavy-hearted, because her father was also her friend.

Jack watched her at a distance. It did not occur to him that the girl's mother was already pitching him at the girl's head, daily and almost hourly, until she was weary of the very sound of his name. And though he felt he must have overstepped some mark in the matter of the flowers, he little dreamt how Miss Sellwood's maid had looked when she saw them, or what disgraceful satisfaction Lady Caroline had exhibited before her daughter on that occasion. He only knew that her Ladyship was treating him with a rather oppressive kindness, and that he would much sooner have had half-a-dozen words from Olivia, such as the first she had ever spoken to him.

And now the girl was unhappy; it was plain enough, even to his untutored eye; and he stepped forward with the determination of improving her spirits, without thinking of his own, which were not a little flat.

"You must find it dull up the country, Miss Sellwood, after London," began Jack, not perhaps in his most natural manner. "I — I wish to goodness you'd tell us of anything we could do to amuse you!"

"You are very good," replied Olivia, "but I don't require to be amused like a child. Thanks all the same. As to finding the country dull, I never appreciate it so much as after a season in town."

She was not looking at the Duke, but beyond him into the hall. And encountering no other eyes there, her own grew softer, as did her tone, even as she spoke.

"You know this old place off by heart, Miss Sellwood, I expect?" pursued Jack, who had taken off his straw hat in her presence, being in doubt as to whether the portico ranked indoors or out.

“Oh, well, I have stayed here pretty often, you know,” said Olivia. “What do you think of the place?”

“I can’t hardly say. I’ve never seen anything else like it. It’s far too good, though, for a chap like me; it’s all so grand.”

“I have sometimes felt it a little too grand,” the girl ventured to observe.

“So. have I!” cried Jack. “You can’t think how glad I am to hear you say that. It’s my own feeling right down to the ground!”

“I don’t mean to be rude,” continued Olivia confidentially, seeing that they were still unobserved, “but I have often felt that I wouldn’t care to live here altogether.”

“No?” said the Duke, in a new tone; he felt vaguely dashed, but his manner was rather one of apologetic sympathy.

“No,” she repeated; “shall you like it?”

“Can’t say. I haven’t weakened on it yet, though it *is* too fine and large for a fellow. Shall I tell you what I’ve done? I’ve fixed up a little place for myself outside, where I can go whenever I get full up of the homestead here. I wonder — if it isn’t too much to ask — whether you would let me show you the little spot I mean?”

“Where is it?”

"In the pines yonder, on the far side o' the tank."

"The tank!"

"We call 'em tanks in Australia. I meant the lake. I could row you across, Miss Sellwood, in a minute, if only you'd let me!" And he met her doubtful look with one of frank, simple-hearted, irresistible entreaty.

"Come on!" said Olivia suddenly; and as she went, she never looked behind; for she seemed to feel her mother's eyes upon her from an upper window, and the hot shame of their certain approval made her tingle from head to foot. So she trod the close, fine, sunlit grass as far as possible from her companion's side. And he, falling back a little, was enabled to watch her all the way.

Olivia was very ordinarily attired. She wore a crisp white blouse, speckled with tiny scarlet spots, and a plain skirt of navy blue, just short enough to give free play to the small brown shoes whose high heels the Duke had admired in the portico. Two scarlet bands, a narrow and a broad, encircled her straw hat and her waist, with much the same circumference: and yet this exceedingly average costume struck Jack as the most delicious thing imaginable of its kind. He corrected another impression before they reached the lake. Olivia was taller than he had thought; she was at least five-feet-six; and she carried her slim, trim figure in a fine upstanding fashion that took some of the roundness out of his own shoulders as he noted it this August morning.

"It's the back-block bend," he remarked elliptically, in the boat.

His way with the oars was inelegant enough, without a pretence at feathering; but it was quite effectual; and Olivia, in the stern-sheets, had her back still presented to the Argus-eyes of the Towers. She answered him with a puzzled look, as well she might, for he had done no more than think aloud.

"What is that?" she said. "And what are the back-blocks; and what *do* you mean?" for her puzzled look had lifted on a smile.

"I was thinking of my round shoulders. You get them through being all your time in the saddle, up in the back-blocks. All the country in Riverina — that is, all the fenced country — is split up into ten-mile blocks. And the back-blocks are the farthest from the rivers and from civilisation. So that's why they call it the back-block bend; it came into my head through seeing you. I never saw anybody hold themselves so well, Miss Sellwood — if it isn't too like my cheek to say so!"

The keel grounded as he spoke, and Olivia, as he handed her out, saw the undulating battlements and toppling turrets of the olden pile upside-down in the tremulous mirror of the lake. A moment later the pine-trees had closed around her; and, sure enough, in a distant window, Lady Caroline Sellwood lowered her opera-glasses with a sigh of exceeding great contentment.

"So you haven't forgotten your old life yet," said the girl, as they stepped out briskly across the shortening shadows of the pines. "I wish you would tell me something about it! I have heard it said that you lived in ever such a little hut, away by yourself in the wilderness."

"I did so; and in a clump of pines the dead spit of these here," said Jack, with a relish. "When I saw these pines you can't think how glad I was! They were like old friends to me; they made me feel at home. You see, Miss Sellwood, that old life is the only one I ever knew, bar this; often enough it seems the reallest of the two. Most nights I dream I'm out there again; last night, for instance, we were lamb-marking. A nasty job, that; I was covered with blood from head to heels, and I was just counting the poor little beggars' tails, when one of the dead tails wriggled in my hand, and blowed if it wasn't Livingstone's! No, there's no forgetting the old life; I was at it too long; it's this one that's most like a dream."

"And the hut," said Olivia, with a rather wry face; "what sort of a place was that?"

"I'll show you," replied the Duke, in what struck the other as a superfluously confidential tone. "It was a little bit of a place, all one room, with a galvanised iron roof and mother-earth for floor. It was built with the very pines that had been felled to make a clearing for the hut: so many uprights, and horizontal slabs in between. A great square hearth and chimney were built out at one end, like the far end of a church; and over my bunk I'd got a lot of pictures from the *Australasian Sketcher* just stuck up anyhow; and if you weren't looking, you knocked your head against the ration-bags that hung from the cross-beams. You slept inside, but you kept your bucket and basin on a bench —— "

"Good heavens!" cried Olivia. And she stood rooted to the ground before a clearing and a hut which exactly tallied with the Duke's description. The hut was indeed too new, the maker's stamp catching the eye on the galvanised roofing; and, in the clearing, the pine-stumps were still white from the axe; but the

essentials were the same, even to the tin basin
on the bench outside the door, with a bucket of
water underneath. As for the wooden chimney,
Olivia had never seen such a thing in her life;
yet real smoke was leaking out of it into the
pale blue sky.

"Is this a joke or a trick?" asked the girl,
looking suspiciously on Jack.

"Neither; it's meant for the dead image of
my old hut up the bush; and it's the little place
I've fixed up for myself, here on the run, that I
wanted to show you."

"You've had it built during these last few
weeks?"

"Under my own eye; and bits of it with my
own hand. Old Claude thought it sheer cussed-
ness, I know; perhaps you will, too; but come
in, and have a look for yourself."

And unlocking the padlock that secured it,
he opened the door and stood aside for the
young girl to enter. Olivia did so with alacrity;
her first amazement had given way to undi-
luted interest; and the Duke followed her,
straw hat in hand. There was a tantalising
insufficiency of light within. Two small windows there were, but both had been filled with
opaque folds of sackcloth in lieu of glass; yet
the Duke pointed to them, as might his ances-

tors to the stained-glass lights in chapel and library, with peculiar pride; and, indeed, his strange delight in the hut, who cared so little for the Towers close at hand, made Olivia marvel when she came to think about it. Meanwhile she found everything as she had heard it described in the Australian hut, with one exception: there were no ration-bags to knock one's head against, because nobody made meals here. Also the pictures over the bunk were from the *Illustrated London News*, not from the *Sketcher*, which Jack had been unable to obtain in England; and they were somewhat unconvincingly clean and well-arranged. But the bunk itself was all that it might have been in the real bush; for it was covered over with Jack's own old blanket; whereon lay a purring, yellow ball, like a shabby sand-bank in a sea of faded blue.

"So this is Livingstone!" exclaimed the girl, stooping to scratch that celebrity's head.

"Yes; and there's old Tom and Black Maria in front of the fire. I lock them all three up during the day, for it isn't so like the bush in some ways as it is in others. They might get stolen any day, with so many people about; that's the worst of the old country; there was no other camp within five miles of me, on Carara."

"It must have been dreadfully lonely!"

"You get used to it. And then every few months you would tramp into the homestead and — and speak to the boss," said Jack, changing his mind and his sentence as he remembered how he had once shocked Claude Lafont.

Olivia took notice of the cats, at which Jack stood by beaming. The kitten she had brought down from town in a basket. It lived in Olivia's room, but she now suggested restoring it to its own people. Jack, however, reminded her that it was hers, in such a tender voice; and proceeded to refer to her kindness at their first meeting, in so embarrassing a fashion; that the girl, seeking a change of subject, found one in the long, low bunk.

"I see," said she, "that you come here for your afternoon siesta."

"I come here for my night's sleep," he replied.

"Never!"

"Every night in life. You seem surprised. I did ask old Claude not to mention it — and — oh, well, it's no use keeping the thing a secret, after all. It suits me best — the open country and the solitude. It's what I'm accustomed to. The wind in the pines all around, I wake up and hear it every night, just like I did in the old hut. It's almost the same thing as going back to the bush to sleep; there's not two penn'orth of difference."

"You'd like to go back altogether," said the girl, affirming it as a fact; and yet her sweet eyes, gravely unsatisfied, seemed to peer through his into his soul.

"I don't say that, Miss Sellwood," he protested. "Of course it's a great thing for me to have come in for all this fortune and power — and it'll be a greater thing still once I can believe it's true! That's the trouble. The whole show's so like a dream. And that's where this little hut helps me; *it's* real, anyway; I can sight *it*. As for all the rest, it's too many measles for me — as yet; what's more, if I was to wake up this minute on Carara I shouldn't so very much mind."

"I wonder," said Olivia, with her fine eyes looking through him still. "I just wonder!" And her tone set him wondering too.

"Of course," he faltered, "I should be mighty sorry to wake up and find I'd only dreamt *you!*"

"Of course," she returned, with a laughing bow; but there had been an instant's pause; and she was studying the picture-gallery over the bunk when she continued, "I see you've been long enough in England to acquire the art of making pretty speeches. And I must tell you at once that they never amuse me. At least," she added more kindly, again facing him, " not when they come from a person as a rule so candid as yourself."

" But you mistake me ; I was perfectly candid," protested poor Jack.

" It won't do," said the girl. " And it's time we went."

Olivia felt that she had made excellent friends with the Duke ; that the more she saw of him, the better she would probably like him ; and that she could possibly be of use to him, in little ways, if he would be sensible, and make no more than a friend of her. She was not so sure of him, however, as she could have wished ; and she was anxious to leave well alone. It was thus the worst of luck that at this last moment she should perceive the suggestively white bouquet upon the high deal chimney-piece.

" You've been to a wedding," she cried, " and I've never heard a word about it ! Whose was the wedding ? Some of the tenantry, of course, or the bride would hardly have presented you with her bouquet !"

And she reached it down, and widened her pretty nostrils over the fading flowers ; but they smelt of death ; and their waxen whiteness had here and there the tarnish of a half-eaten apple.

"There was no bride," said Jack, "and no wedding."

"Then why this bride's bouquet? No! I beg your pardon; it isn't a fair question."

"It is — perfectly. I had it made for a young lady. The head-gardener made it, but I told him first what I wanted. There was no word of a wedding; I only thought a nosegay would be the right sort of thing to give a young lady, to show her she was mighty welcome; and I thought white was a nice clean sort of colour. But it turned out I was wrong; she wouldn't have liked it; it would only have made her uncomfortable; so, when I found out that, I just let it rest."

"I see," said Olivia, seeing only too clearly. "Still, I'm not sure you were right: if I had been the girl ——"

"Yes?"

The quick word altered the speech it had also interrupted.

"I should have thought it exceedingly kind of you," said Olivia, after a moment's reflection.

She replaced the flowers on the chimney-board, and then led the way out among the pines.

"I'm sorry you were in such a hurry," he said, overtaking her when he had locked up the hut. "I might have made you some billy-tea. The billy's the can you make it in up the bush. I had such a work to get one over here! I keep some tea in the hut, and billy-tea's not like any other kind; I call it better; but you must come again and sample it for yourself."

" We'll see," said Olivia smilingly; but with that she lost her tongue; and together they crossed the lake in mutually low spirits. It was as though the delicate spell of simple friendship had been snapped as soon as spun between them, and the friends were friends no more.

On the lawn, however, in a hammock under an elm, they found a young man smoking. It was Mr. Edmund Stubbs, who had arrived, with his friend the Impressionist, on the Saturday afternoon. He was smoking a pipe; but the ground beneath him was defiled with the ends of many cigarettes; and close at hand a deck-chair stood empty.

"I smell the blood of Mr. Llewellyn," said Olivia, coming up with the glooming Duke. " He smokes far too many cigarettes!"

" He has gone for more," said the man in the hammock.

“I wonder you don’t interfere, Mr. Stubbs; it must be so bad for him.”

“On the contrary, Miss Sellwood, it is the best thing in the world for him. A man must smoke something. And an artist must smoke cigarettes. You can tell what he does smoke, however, from his work. Pipe-work is inevitably coarse, banal, obvious, and only fit to hang in the front parlours of Brixton and Upper Tooting. Cigar-work is little better; but that of the cigarette is delicate, suggestive, fantastic if you will, but always artistic. Ivor Llewellyn’s is typical cigarette-work.”

“How very interesting,” said Olivia.

“My colonial!” muttered the Duke.

At the same time they caught each other’s eyes, turned away with one consent, nor made a sound between them until they were out of earshot of the hammock. And then they only laughed; yet the spell that had been broken was even thus made whole.

CHAPTER IX

AN ANONYMOUS LETTER

IT is comparatively easy to read a character from a face. This is always a scientific possibility. To fit the face to a given character is obviously the reverse. And those who knew the worst of Lady Caroline Sellwood, before making her acquaintance, received, on that occasion, something like a shock. They had nourished visions of a tall and stately figure with a hook-nose and an exquisitely supercilious smile; whereas her Ladyship was decidedly short, and extremely stout, with as plebeian a snub-nose and as broad a grin as any in her own back-kitchen. Instead of the traditionally frigid leader of society, she was a warm-hearted woman where her own interests were not concerned; where they were, she was just what expedience made her, and her heart then took its temperature from her head, like the excellent servant it had always been. A case very much in point is that of her relations with Claude Lafont, whom, however, Lady Caroline had now her own reasons for fearing no more. As for the Duke of St. Osmund's, her heart had been a perfect oven to him from the first.

Nor did she make any pretence about the matter — it was this that so repelled Olivia. But the very falsity of the woman was frank to the verge of a virtue; and the honest dishonesty of her front hair (which was of the same shade as Olivia's, only much more elaborately curled) was as bluntly emblematic as a pirate's flag. Lady Caroline Sellwood was honestly dishonest to the last ounce of her two hundredweight of avoirdupois.

This was the kind of thing she thought nothing of doing. She had been engaged for months upon an egregious smoking-cap for Claude Lafont. That is to say she had from time to time put in a few golden stitches, in front of Claude, which her maid had been obliged to pick out and put in again behind the scenes. Claude, at any rate, had always understood that the cap was for him — until one evening here in the conservatory, when he saw Lady Caroline coolly trying it on the Duke.

"It never did fit you, Claude," she explained serenely. "It was always too small, and I must make you another. Only see how it fits the dear Duke!"

The dear Duke was made the recipient of many another mark of unblushing favour. He could do no wrong. His every solecism of act or word, and they still cropped up at times, was simply "sweet" in the eyes of Lady Caroline Sellwood, and his name was seldom on her lips without that epithet.

Moreover, she would speak her mind to him on every conceivable topic, and this with a freedom often embarrassing for Jack; as, for example, on the first Sunday after church.

"I simply don't know how Francis dared!" Lady Caroline exclaimed, as she took Jack's arm on the sunlit terrace. "Twenty-one minutes by my watch — and such drivel! It didn't seem so to you? Ah, you're so sweet! But twenty-one minutes was an outrage, and I shall tell the little idiot exactly what I think of him."

"I rather like him," said Jack, who put it thus mildly out of pure politeness to his companion; "and I rather liked what he said."

"Oh, he's no worse than the rest of them," rejoined Lady Caroline. "Of course I swear by the sweet Established Church, but the parsons personally, with very few exceptions, I never could endure. Still, it's useful to have one in the family; he does everything for us.

He christens the grandchildren, and he'll bury
the lot of us if he's spared, to say nothing of
marrying poor Olivia when her time comes.
Ah well, let's hope that won't be yet! She is
my ewe lamb. And all men are not such dear
sweet fellows as you!"

This sort of speech he found unanswerable;
and although treated by her Ladyship with
unflagging consideration, amounting almost to
devotion, Jack was never at his ease in such
interviews.

One of these took place in the hut. Lady
Caroline insisted on seeing it, accompanied by
Olivia. Of course the whole idea charmed her
to ecstasies; it was so original; it showed such
a simple heart; and the hut itself was as
"sweet" as everything else connected with the
Duke. So was the pannikin of tea which Jack
was entreated to brew for her in the "billy":
indeed, this was too sweet for Lady Caroline,
who emptied most of hers upon the earth behind
her camp-stool — an act which Jack pretended
not to detect, and did not in the least resent.
On the contrary, he put a characteristic construction upon the incident, which he attributed exclusively to Lady Caroline's delicate
reluctance to hurt his feelings by expressing
her real opinion of the tea; for though per-

sonally oppressed by her persistent kindness, he was much too unsophisticated, and had perhaps too good a heart of his own, ever to suspect an underlying motive.

Towards the end of that week, in fact on the Friday afternoon, they were all taking tea on the terrace; or rather all but the two talented young men, who were understood never to touch it, and who, indeed, were somewhat out of their element at the Towers, except late at night, when the ladies had gone to bed. "I can't think why you asked them down," said Lady Caroline to Claude. "I didn't," was the reply; "it was you, Jack." "Of course it was me," cried the astonished Jack, "and why not? Didn't they use to go to your rooms, old man, and to your house, Lady Caroline?" "Ah," said her Ladyship, with her indulgent smile, "but that was rather a different thing — you dear kind fellow!" All this, however, was not on the Friday afternoon, when Lady Caroline was absorbed in very different thoughts. They were not of the conversation, although she put in her word here and there; the subject, that of the Nottingham murder, being one of peculiar interest. The horrible case in question, which had filled the papers all that week, had ended the previous day in an inevitable conviction. And even Claude was moved to the expression of a strong opinion as he put down the *Times*.

"I must say that I agree with the judge," he remarked with a shudder. "'Unparalleled barbarity' is the only word for it! What on earth, though, was there to become 'almost inaudible with emotion' about, in passing sentence? If I could see any man hanged with equanimity, or indeed at all, I confess it would be this loathly wretch."

"Claude," said Lady Caroline, "I'm ashamed of you. He is an innocent man. He shall not die."

"Who's to prevent it?" asked Jack.

"I am," replied Lady Caroline calmly.

"There'll probably be a petition, you see," exclaimed Claude. "Then the Home Secretary decides."

"And I decide the Home Secretary," said Lady Caroline Sellwood.

It was grossly untrue, and Olivia shook her head in answer to the Duke's astounded stare, but her mother's eyes were again fixed thoughtfully on lawn and lake. The short dry grass was overrun with wild thyme, innumerable butterflies played close to it, as spray, and the air hummed with bees likewise in love with the aroma, whose fragrance reached even to the terrace. But Lady Caroline noted none of these things, nor yet the shadows of spire and turret encroaching on the lawn — nor yet the sunlight strong as ever on the lake beyond. She was already pondering on the best way of bringing a certain matter to a head. This quiet country life, with so tiny a house-party, and with one day so like another, was excellent so far as it went, but the chances were that it would not go the whole way. It lacked excitement and incentive. It was the kind of life in which an attachment might too easily stagnate in mere foolish friendship. It needed an event; a something to prepare for, to look forward to; a something to tighten the nerves and slacken the tongue; and yet nothing that should give the Duke an opportunity of appearing at a public disadvantage.

So this was the difficulty. It disqualified the dance, the dinner-party, even the entertaining of the county from 3.30 to 6.30 in the grounds. But Lady Caroline overcame it, as she overcame most difficulties, by the patient application of her ingenious mind. And her outward scheme was presently unfolded in the fewest and apparently the most spontaneous words.

" He is not guilty, and he shall not die," she suddenly observed, as though the Nottingham murder had all this time monopolised her thoughts. "But let us speak of something else; I had, indeed, a very different matter upon my mind, until the papers came and banished everything with this ghastly business. The fact is, dear Duke, that you should really do something to entertain your tenantry, and possibly a few neighbours also, before they begin to talk. They will expect it sooner or later, and in these things it is always better to take time by the forelock. Mind, I don't mean an elaborate matter at all — except from their point of view. I would just give them the run of the place for the afternoon, and feed the multitude later on. Francis, don't look shocked! I hope you'll be there to ask a blessing. Then, Duke, you could have a band on the lawn, and fireworks, and indeed anything you like. It's always good policy to do the civil to one's tenantry, though no doubt a bore; but you needn't shake hands with them, you know, and you could leaven the lower orders with a few parsons and their wives·from the surrounding rectories. It's only a suggestion, of course, and that from one who has really no right to put in her oar at all; still I know you won't misunderstand it — coming from *me*."

He did not; his face had long been **alight**

and aglow with the red-heat of his enthusiasm ; and now his words leapt forth like flames.

"The very ticket!" he cried, starting to his feet. "A general muster of all sorts, and we'll do 'em real well. Fizz and fireworks! A dance on the lawn! And I'll make 'em a speech to wind up with!"

"That would be beautiful," said Lady Caroline with an inward shudder. "What a dear fellow you are, to be sure, to take up my poor little suggestion like this!"

"Take it up," cried Jack, "I should think I would take it up! It'll be the best sport out. Lady Caroline, you're one in two or three! I'm truly thankful for the tip. Here's my hand on it!"

His hand was pressed without delay.

"It really is an excellent suggestion," said Claude Lafont, in his deliberate way, after mature consideration. "It only remains to settle the date."

"And the brand of fizz, old man, and the sort of fireworks! I'll leave all that to you. And the date, too; any day will do me; the sooner the better."

"Well," said Lady Caroline, as though it had only just struck her, "Olivia's birthday is the twentieth——"

“ Mamma ! ” cried that young lady, with real indignation.

“ And it’s her twenty-first birthday,” pursued the other, “ and she is my ewe lamb.   I must confess I should like to honour that occasion —— ”

“ Same here !   By all manner o’ means ! ” broke in the Duke.   “ Now, Miss Sellwood, it’s no use your saying one word ; this thing’s a fixture for the twentieth as ever is.”

The girl was furious.   The inevitable, nay, the intentional linking of her name with that of the Duke of St. Osmund’s, entailed by the arrangement thus mooted and made, galled her pride to the quick.   And yet it was but one more twang of the catapult that was daily and almost hourly throwing her at his head ; neither was it his fault any more than hers ; so she made shift to thank him, as kindly as she could at the moment, for the compliment he was so ready to pay her — at her mother’s suggestion.

“ You could hardly get out of it, however, after what was said,” she added, not perhaps inexcusably in the circumstances.

“ No more can you,” retorted the Duke. “ And here comes the very man we must all consult,” he added, as the agent appeared, a taking figure in his wrinkled riding breeches, and with his spurs trailing on the dead-smooth flags.

The agent handed Jack a soiled note, and then sat down to talk to the ladies. This he did at all times excellently, having assurance and a certain well-bred familiarity of manner, which, as the saying is, went down. In this respect he was a contrast to all the other men present. He inquired when the Home Secretary would be back and ready for his revenge on the links. And he heard of the plans for the twentieth with interest and a somewhat superfluous approval. Meanwhile the Duke had read his note more than once, and now he looked up.

"Where did you get this?" he asked, displaying the crumpled envelope, which had also a hole through the middle.

"In rather a rum place," replied the agent. "It was nailed to a tree just outside the north gates."

"Well, see here," said Jack, who stood facing the party, with his back to the stone bulwark of the terrace, and a hard look on his face; "that's just the sort of place where I should have expected you to find it, for it's an anonymous letter that some fellows might keep to themselves — but not me! I'm for getting to the bottom of things, whether they're nice or whether they're nasty. Listen to this: ' To the DUKE of St. Osmund's ' — he prints ' Duke ' in big letters, as much as to say I'm not one. ' A word in your GRACE'S ear ' — he prints that the same. ' They say,' he says, ' that you hail from Australia, and *I* say you're not the first claimant to titles and estates that has sprung from there. Take a friendly tip and put on as few frills as possible till you're quite sure you are not going to be bowled out for a second Tichborne. A WELL-WISHER.' Now what does it all mean? Is it simple cheek, or isn't it? I recollect all about Tichborne. I recollect seeing him in Wagga when I was a lad, and we took a great interest in his case up the bush; but why am I like him? Where does the likeness come in? I've heard fat men called second Tichbornes, but I don't turn twelve stone. Then what can he mean? Does he mean I'm not a Duke? I know I'm not fit to be one; but that's another matter; and if it comes to that, I never claimed to be one either; it was Claude here who yarded me up into this pen! Then what's it all about? Can any lady or gentleman help me? I'll pass the letter round, and I'll be mightily obliged if they can!"

They could: it was pure insolence, not to be

taken seriously for a single moment. So they
all said with one consent; and Jack was further
advised to steel himself forthwith against anonymous letters, of which persons in his station received hundreds every year. The agent added
that he believed he knew who had written this
one; at least he had his suspicions.

In a word, the affair was treated by all in the
very common-sense light of a mere idle insult;
any serious sympathy that was evinced being due
entirely to the fact that Jack himself seemed
to take it rather to heart. Lady Caroline Sellwood dismissed the matter with the fewest
words of all; nevertheless, Jack detected her
in a curious, penetrating, speculative scrutiny
of himself, which he could not fathom at the
time; and her Ladyship had a word to say to
Claude Lafont after obtaining his arm as far as
the house.

" That sort of thing is never pleasant," she
observed confidentially, "and I can't help wishing the dear fellow had kept his letter to himself. It gives one such disagreeable ideas! I
am the last person to be influenced by such
pieces of impudence, as a general rule; still I
could not help thinking what a very awkward
thing it would be if your Mr. Cripps had made
a big mistake after all! Not awkward from

every point of view, dear Claude" — and here she pressed his arm — "but — but of course he had every substantial proof?"

"Of course," said Claude. "I looked into it, as a matter of form, on Cripps's return; though his word was really quite sufficient. Well, he had copies of the certificate of Jack's birth, and of that of my uncle's marriage, besides proof positive that Jack was Jack. And that was good enough for me."

"And for me too," said Lady Caroline, dropping his arm. "He is a dear fellow; I hardly know which is greater, my regard for him or my sympathy with you!" And her Ladyship marched upstairs.

Meantime the agent had led Jack aside on the terrace.

"I know who sent that letter," said he. "I had my suspicions all along, and I recognised the disguised hand in a moment. It was Matthew Hunt."

"Well?" said Jack.

"Well, it was meant merely as an annoyance: a petty revenge for the handsome thrashing you gave the fellow six weeks ago — I wish I'd seen it! But that's not the point. The point is that I think I could bring it home to the brute; and I want your Grace to let me try."

"I can't. What's the good? Leave bad alone; we should only make it worse."

"Then mayn't I raise the rent of the Lower Farm?"

"No; not yet, at any rate. I mean to give the fellow a chance."

"And an invitation for the twentieth too?"

"Certainly; he's a tenant, or his father is; we can't possibly leave them out."

"Very well; your Grace knows best."

And the agent went his way.

CHAPTER X

"DEAD NUTS"

IT was three o'clock in the early morning of
the twentieth of August. A single jet of gas,
lighting a torch in the mailed hand of a life-
size man-at-arms, burnt audibly in the silent
hall; making the worst of each lugubrious
feature, like a match struck in a cavern. And
Claude Lafont was sitting up alone, in the
Poet's Corner, at work upon his birthday offering to Olivia Sellwood.

At three, however, it was finished in the
rough. The poet then stretched his fingers,
took a clean sheet of paper, and started upon
the fair copy in his prettiest hand. It began —

> " What songs have I to sing you?
> What tales have I to tell?"   '

And there it stuck, as though these questions
were indeed unanswerable; the fact being, there
was another still to come, which, however, in-
volved an execrable couplet as it stood. Claude

twisted it about for half-an-hour; realised its gratuitous badness; tried not to ask this inane question at all, hunted his rhyming dictionary up and down, and found he must; and finally, with a prayer that it might impose upon Olivia, and another for forgiveness from the Muse, finished his first stanza with—

> " What garlands can I bring you
> From Fancy's fairest dell?
> Before the world grew old, dear,
> The lute was lightlier strung;
> Now all the tales are told, dear,
> And all the songs are sung."

It is needless to quote more. The sentiments were superior to their setting. An affectionate *camaraderie* was employed, with success, as a cloak for those warmer feelings of whose existence in his own bosom the poor poet was now practically convinced. And the lines in themselves were not all or wholly bad; there was a certain knack in them, and here and there some charm. But if infinite pains could have made them a work of genius, that they would have been. It was almost five when Claude made his best signature at the foot of the last verse; yet there were but four of these, or thirty-two lines in all.

He put them in an envelope which he sealed deliberately with his signet-ring. The deliberation of all his private doings was enormous; neither the hour nor an empty stomach could induce briskness at the expense of pains. Yet Claude was exceedingly hungry, and the night had put an edge on his nerves. As he paced the floor the undue distinction between his steps, so soft on the rugs, and so loud on the parquetry, became exaggerated in his nervous ears; and all the silence and all the darkness of the sleeping Towers seemed to press upon that single lamp-lit, sounding room, like fathoms of wide sea upon a diver's helm. Claude had not thought of such things while he was still at work; he had rather overdone matters, and he poured out a sparing measure of whisky from the decanter upon the table.

There were other glasses with dregs at the bottom. The air was tainted with stale smoke, and within the fender lay the remains of many cigarettes. This was why Claude was so late. He had been late in making a start. Stubbs and Llewellyn had sat up with him till the small hours. The Poet's Corner was the one spot in which these young men seemed really at home. Here, by midnight, but seldom before, they could manage to create unto themselves their own element; for their Philistine host went early to his eccentric lair; but there were always his easy-chairs to lounge in, his whisky to drink, and Claude Lafont to listen to their talk.

Not that the poet was so good a listener as he had been once; the truth being, that he found himself a little out of touch with his clever friends — he hardly knew why. It might be the living under one roof with them; he himself would never have asked them down. Or it might be the simultaneous hourly contact with an opposite type of man — the kindly, unaffected dunce — the unburnished nugget, reeking yet of the Australian soil, but with the gold wearing brighter every day.

Certain it was that the benefit of the cousins' close companionship had not been all on one side. If the force of example had toned down some of Jack's pristine roughness of speech and manner, it had taken a like effect upon sundry peculiarities of a converse character in Claude. In a word, there had been an ideal interchange between the two, founded on a mutual liking. The ameliora-tion of the Duke was sufficiently obvious to all; that of Claude struck Olivia especially, who had never been blind to his faults; needless to add, he was himself the last to see how he had changed. Yet he divined something of it now. As he

thought of the verses he had just written, and of
the critic to whom he would have submitted
them in all humility a couple of months ago,
he knew that he was no longer as he had been
then; for he had not the faintest intention of
allowing that critic to see these verses at all.

So Claude calmed his nerves, eating biscuits
the while, and sipping soda-water merely tinct-
ured with whisky; until all at once the lamp
began to flicker and to smell, and the song of
the birds, singing in Olivia's birthday, came at
last to his ears through the plate-glass and rich
curtains of the octagonal window. Then he rose;
and in half a minute the lamp was out, the curtains drawn, a sash thrown up, and the risen sun
shining mercilessly on the dishevelled head and
blue chin and battered shirt-front of Claude
Lafont.

The cool, fresh scene inspired him with delight; it was indeed a disgraceful novelty to the
poet. He thought nothing of rhyming "morn"
with "dawn," and yet of this phenomenon itself
he had little or no experience. He would gain
some now; he also promised himself the unique
pleasure of rousing the early-rising Jack. So
he got out of the window, and soaked his feet
in the dew, only to meet Jack emerging from
his hut, with towels on his arm, as he approached

it. Nor was the Duke's surprise very flattering; but his chaff was fair enough. He was himself about to bathe in the creek at the north end of the tank. Would Claude join him and then go back to the hut for an early pannikin of bush tea? Claude would, and did, feeling (as all felt at Jack's hut) that he had been flashed through the thick of the earth, and come out in the wilds of Australia.

In the hut a log fire had burnt well up by the time they returned with wet towels and glowing skins. Over the flames hung the billy-can, with boiling water throbbing against the side. Jack lifted it down with a stick, and threw a handful of tea among the bubbles. "Shall I sweeten it?" he then asked; and, at Claude's nod, threw in another handful of brown sugar.

"There, that's real bush tea for you," continued the Duke, in a simmer of satisfaction himself as he stirred the mixture with the stick. "Now take the pannikin and dip it in. There's no milk, mind; that wouldn't be the thing at all. Here are some biscuits, and they aren't the thing either. I'd have made you a damper, only I never could strike a camp-oven; it's been trouble enough to raise the plant I've got. What do you think of the tea?"

"Capital!" cried Claude, who was seated on

the bunk.   And indeed the whole thing appealed
to his poetic palate; for he could not forget that
this hut was within half a mile of the Towers
themselves, in which the Duke took evidently
far less pleasure; and the many-sided contrast
amused his literary sense, even while it piqued
his family pride.

"How I wish it was the real thing!" said
Jack, with a sigh. "I'd have a camp-oven, then,
and you should have your mutton chop and
damper served up hot.   I used to be an artist at
a damper.   Then after breakfast I'd take you
with me round the paddocks, and you'd help me
muster a mob and drive them to the tank; and
you'd hear them bleat and see them start to run
when they smelt the water.   My colonial oath,
I can see 'em and hear 'em now!   Then we'd
give our mokes a drink in the middle of 'em,
and we'd take a pull at our own water-bags.
Then we might camp under the nearest hop-bush
for a snack, and I should yard you up at the
homestead, and make you know my old boss
before the day was over.   What a day it would
be for you!   You wouldn't believe the sky
could get so blue or your face so red.   But it's
no use talking — here we are again!"   And he
set down his empty pannikin with another sigh.

"You wouldn't really prefer that life to this?"

"No; perhaps not; but I like to think of it, as you can see."

"Surely you like your new life best by this time? You wouldn't go back there now?"

"I like my new friends best; I wouldn't go back on them. Olivia and you, for instance."

"It's her birthday," said Claude; but a silence had intervened.

"So it is. God bless her! I haven't got her anything, because I seemed to make a mull of it with those flowers. Have you?"

"Yes, I have a trifle for her; it's rather a different thing on her birthday, you know. And —and I've written her a few verses; that's what I've been doing all night."

"Clever dog!" said Jack enviously. "See what it is to be a man of genius; here's where it comes in so handy. And has Llewellyn done her something, too?"

"Yes; a portrait of herself."

"Well, let him label it to that effect, or she may put her foot in it like me. He never shows me his blooming drawings now. But I wish you'd let me see your poem."

"It's not all that; it's only verses, and pretty bad ones too; still, you shall hear them if you like, and if I can remember them," said Claude, who would have found much more difficulty in forgetting them so soon. "I only wish they were better! There are some lamentable lines here and there. I tried to iron them out, but they wouldn't all come."

"Go on!" cried Jack, lighting his pipe. "I'll tell you whether they're good or bad. You go ahead!"

And Claude did so, only too glad of a second opinion of any kind; for he had little or no intellectual self-reliance, and was ever ready to think his productions good or bad with their latest critic. On this occasion, however, he would have been better pleased with the general enthusiasm of the Duke, had not the latter proceeded to point out particular merits, when it transpired that the ingenuity of the rhymes was what impressed him most. Knowing where they came from, the poet himself was unable to take much pride in this feature.

"They're splendid!" reiterated Jack. "You ought to be the laureate, old man, and I've a good mind to tell 'em so in the House of Lords. You're far and away ahead of Shakespeare at rhyming; he hardly ever rhymes at all; I know that; because there used to be a copy of him in my old hut. I say, I like that about the garlands from Fancy's dell; that's real poetry, that is. But do you mind giving me the last four lines again?"

Claude gave them—

> "While yet the world was young, dear,
>   Your minstrel might be bold:
> Now all the songs are sung, dear,
>   And all the tales are told."

"First-chop," said Jack, whose look, however, was preoccupied. "But what's that you're driving at about the minstrel being bolder? What was it you'd have said if only you'd had the cheek? Say it to me. Out with it!"

"I don't know, really," said Claude, laughing.

"Then I do: you're dead nuts on Olivia!"

"What's that?"

"You like her!"

"Naturally."

"As much as I do!"

"That all depends how much you like her, Jack."

There was a moment's pause. The Duke was sitting on his heels in front of the fire, into which he was also staring fixedly; so that it was impossible to tell whether the red light upon his face was spontaneous or reflected. And he spoke out now without turning his head.

"Old man," he said, "I've wanted a straight word with you this long time — about Olivia. Of course I know I oughtn't to call her Olivia behind her back, when I daren't to her face; but that's what she is in my own heart, you see — and that's where she's pegged out a claim for good and all. Understand? We can't all talk like books, old man! Still I want to make myself as plain as possible."

"You do so. I understand perfectly," said Claude Lafont.

"That's all right. Well, as I was saying, she's pegged out a claim that no other woman is ever going to jump. And what I was going to say was this: you remember that night in your rooms in town? I mean when I said I meant no harm, and all that; because I spoke too soon. Worse still, I felt mean when I did speak; it didn't ring true; and long I've known that even then there was only one thing that would have held me back. That was — if she'd been your girl! I gave you a chance of saying if she was, but you only laughed; and sometimes I've thought your laugh wasn't any truer than my word. So I've got to have it in plain English before I go the whole hog. Claude — old man — she never was — your girl?"

"Never," said Claude decidedly.

"You never asked her — what I think of asking one of these days?"

"Never."

"Thank God, old man. I'm dead nuts on her myself, I tell you frankly; and I mean to tell *her* when I can rake together the pluck. I'm not sure I can keep it to myself much longer. The one thing I'm sure of is that she'll laugh in my face — if she isn't too riled! I hear her doing it every night of my life as I lie where you're sitting and listen to the pines outside. I hear her saying every blessed thing but 'yes!' Yet it isn't such cheek as all that, is it, Claude? I want your candid opinion. I'm not such a larrikin as I was that day you met me, am I?"

And he turned to the other with a simple, strong humility, very touching in him; but Claude jumped up, and getting behind him so that their eyes should not meet, laid his hands affectionately on the Duke's shoulders.

"You are not the same man," he said with a laugh; "yet you are the same good fellow! I could wish Olivia no better fate — than the one you think of. So I wish you luck — from my heart. And now let us go."

On the lawn they found the Home Secretary driving a dozen golf-balls into space from an impromptu tee. He had come for good now, the session being over at last. And this was his daily exercise before breakfast, and his valet's daily grievance, whose duty it was to recover the balls.

Mr. Sellwood accompanied the younger men into the house, where Claude had still to shave and dress; but the Duke was the uninterested witness of an interesting scene, between the Home Secretary and his wife, before any one else came down to breakfast. The subject was that of the Nottingham murder.

"They are making an example of you!" said Lady Caroline bitterly, looking up from her husband's daily stack of press-cuttings, which she always opened.

"Let them," said Mr. Sellwood, from the depths of the *Sportsman*, which he read before any of his letters.

"They call it a judicial murder—and upon my word, so do I! Your decision is most unpopular; they clamour for your resignation —and I must say that I should do the same. Here's a cartoon of you playing golf with a human skull for the ball!"

"Exactly how I mean to spend my day—barring the skull."

"They know it, too; it's a public scandal; even if it wasn't, I should be ashamed of myself, with that poor man awaiting his end!"

"He was hanged five minutes ago," declared the Home Secretary, consulting his watch. "And I may as well tell you, my dear, that I had his full confession in my pocket when I gave my decision the night before last. It appears in this morning's papers. And I fancy that's my hole," added Mr. Sellwood, nodding at Jack.

But Jack had no more to say than Lady Caroline, utterly routed for once. The Duke did not perhaps appreciate the situation, or perhaps he was not listening; for his eyes hung very wistfully on Olivia's plate, which was laden and surrounded by birthday offerings of many descriptions. There were several packets by post, and an open cheque from the Home Secretary. Claude had added his beautifully sealed envelope before going upstairs, and now Llewellyn came in with his "likeness of a lady." The lady was evidently lost in a fog; the likeness did not exist; and the whole production was exactly like a photographic failure which is both out of focus and "over-exposed." But it was better than poor Jack's contribution of nothing at all.

CHAPTER XI

THE NIGHT OF THE TWENTIETH

A LOOSE chain of fairy lights marked the brink of the lake; another was drawn tight from end to end of the balustrade rimming the terrace; and between the two, incited by champagne and the Hungarian band, the rank and file of the tenantry cut happy capers in the opening eye of the harvest moon.

At one end of the terrace the fire-workers awaited the word to rake and split the still serenity of the heavens; at the other, the fairy footlights picked out the twinkling diamonds and glaring shirt-fronts of the house-party, the footmen's gilt buttons and powdered heads; for the men had just come out of the dining-room, and tea was being handed round.

"It is going beautifully — beautifully!" whispered Lady Caroline, swooping down upon the Duke, who had himself made straight for her daughter's side. "Inside and out, high and low, all are happy, it is one huge success. How could it be otherwise? You make such a charming host! My dear Jack, I congratulate you from my heart; and the occasion must be my excuse for the familiarity."

"No excuse needed; I like it," replied the Duke. "I only wish you'd all call me Jack," he added, with a sidelong look at Olivia; "surely we're all pretty much in the same family boat! Well, I'm glad you think it's a success, and I'm glad I make a decent host; but I shouldn't if I hadn't got the loan of such an excellent hostess, Lady Caroline."

"You are so sweet!"

"Nay, it's you that's so jolly kind," laughed Jack. "The fact is, Lady Caroline, I can get along all right at my own table so long as I don't have to carve — and when I make up my mind to go straight through cold water. I was sorry not to drink Miss Sellwood's health in anything stronger; but it's better so."

"So fine of you," murmured Lady Caroline; "such a noble example! You can't think how I've admired it in you from the first!"

Yet she looked to see whether his remarks had been overheard. They had not; even Olivia had turned away before they were made, and her mother now followed her example. She was rewarded by seeing the Duke at the girl's side again when next she looked round.

They were standing against the balustrade, a little apart from the rest. They had set their cups upon the broad stone rim. Jack began to stir his tea with the impotent emphasis of one possessed by the inexpressible. But Olivia gave him no assistance; she seemed more interested in the noisy dancers on the sward below the terrace.

"I hope you've had a good time, on the whole," he began, ineptly enough, at last. "All this is in your honour, you know!"

"Surely not all," replied the girl, laughing. "Still I don't know when I had such a delightful birthday, and I want to thank you for everything with all my heart."

"Everything!" laughed Jack nervously. "I've done nothing at all; why, I didn't even give you a present. That was through a stupid mistake of mine, which we needn't go into, because now's the time to rectify it. I've been waiting for a chance all the evening. The thing only came a few minutes before dinner. But better late than never, they say, and so I hope you'll still accept this trifle from me, Miss Sellwood, with every possible good wish for all the years to come. May they be long and — and very happy!"

His voice vibrated with the commonplace

words. As he ceased speaking he took from his waistcoat pocket something that was certainly trifling in size, and he set it on the balustrade between the two tea-cups. It was a tiny leathern case, and Olivia held her breath. Next moment an exquisite ring, diamonds and emeralds, scintillated in the light of the nearest fairy lamp.

"This is never for me?" she cried, aghast.

"That it is — if you will take it."

She was deeply moved: how could she take a ring from him? And yet how could she refuse, or how explain! Each alternative was harder than the last.

"It is far too good for me," she murmured, "for a mere birthday present! You are too generous. I can't dream of letting you give me anything half so good!"

"What nonsense! It is not half good enough; it's only the best I could get from Devenholme. I sent in the dogcart for the crack jeweller of the place; it brought him back with a bagful of things, and this was the best of a bad lot. I wish I'd kept the fellow! You might have chosen something else."

She saw her loophole and made no reply.

"Would you prefer something else?" he asked eagerly.

" Well, if you insist on giving me a present, it must be something not half so good."

" That's my affair."

" And perhaps not a ring."

" That's another matter, and on one condition I'm on : you must let me drive you in to-morrow to choose for yourself."

She consented gratefully. Her gratitude was the more profuse from, it may be, an exaggerated sense of the dilemma in which she had found herself a moment before; at all events it was very kindly and charmingly expressed. So Jack pocketed the ring and swallowed his tea in excellent heart; longing already for the morrow, for the expedition to Devenholme with Olivia alone at his side.

" That excellent fellow seems very busy with our Olivia. Is there anything in it? " asked Mr. Sellwood of his wife.

" I have no idea," replied Lady Caroline; " you know I never interfere in such matters. I'm glad you think him an excellent fellow, though. He is simply sweet."

" In fact we might do worse from every point of view; is that it? " said the Home Secretary dryly. " I'm inclined to agree with you. I hope he won't foozle his shot by being in too great a hurry."

The fireworks had begun. Rocket after rocket split the sky and descended in a shower of stars. A set-piece stood out against the lake; it represented six French eagles on a shield.

"Come and have a look at the family fowls," said Jack, rejoining Olivia, who had been talking to Claude. "I'd swop the lot for one respectable emu; it would be a good deal more appropriate for a Duke like me."

Among other things he had learnt at last to pronounce his own title correctly. Also, he looked well at all times in evening dress, but he had never looked better than he did to-night. Claude had these consolations as he watched the pair go down and mingle with the throng.

As a matter of fact the Duke of St. Osmund's had never been in higher spirits in the whole course of his chequered career. Olivia had not, indeed, accepted his offering, but she had done much better, for now he was sure of having her to himself for hours the next day. And what might not happen in those hours? This was one factor in his present content; her little hand within his arm was another that thrilled him even more; but there were further and smaller factors which yet astonished him, each with its unexpected measure of gratification. There were the people bowing and curtseying as he came among them with Olivia on his arm. There were the momentary glimpses of the stately Towers, seen from end to end in a flash, as a bursting rocket spattered the sky with a million sparks that changed colour as they floated to the earth. And there was the feeling, never before this moment entirely unmixed, that after all it was better to be the Duke of St. Osmund's than Happy Jack of New South Wales.

"You were right!" he exclaimed, in an attempt to voice what he felt to Olivia; "you were quite right that day in the hut to say 'I wonder,' to what I said about not minding if I woke up and found myself on Carara after all. You set *me* wondering at the time, and now I rather think that I should mind a good deal. This place grows upon you. I feel it more and more every morning when I get the first glimpse of it, coming through the pines. But I never felt it as I do to-night — look at that!"

The entire front of the building was lit up by an enormous Roman candle, playing like a fountain on the terrace. Turret and spire and battlement were stamped sharp and grey against the darkling sky. The six Corinthian columns of the portico stood out like sentinels who had taken a step forward as one man. And in the tympanum overhead the shield of the six eagles that was carved there showed so plainly that Olivia and Jack pointed it out to each other at the same moment.

"You mustn't think I've no respect for the fowls," said the Duke, when they were both left blinking in the chaste light of the reproving moon; "I'm proud enough of them at the bottom of my heart. I may be slow at catching on to new ideas. I know I didn't at first take to everything like a duck to water. I couldn't, after the life I'd led; it was too much for one man. But I am getting used to it now. As old Claude says, I'm beginning to appreciate it. I am so! This has been the proudest day of my life; I'm proud of everything, of the place, the people——"

"And yourself most of all!" cried a thick voice at his elbow, while Olivia's fingers tightened on his other arm.

It was Matthew Hunt. He was flushed with wine, but steady enough on his legs. Only his tongue was beyond control, and a crowd was at his heels to hear what he would say next.

"Yes, I remember you," he continued savagely. "I shan't forget that morning in a hurry——"

"Yet you seem to have forgotten who you are speaking to," put in the Duke quietly.

Hunt laughed horribly.

"Forgotten? I never knew! All I know is as I'm *not* speaking to his Grace the Duke —— "

Olivia was not shaken off. She only felt a quivering in the arm she held; she only guessed it was the other arm that shot out too quick for her sight from his further shoulder; and all she saw was the dropping of Hunt at their feet, as if with a bullet through his brain. She conquered her impulse to scream, and she found herself saying instead, "Well done! It served him right!" And the voice sounded strange in her own ears.

But her opinion was freely echoed by those who had followed in Hunt's wake. A dozen hands raised him roughly, and kept their hold of him even when he was firm upon his feet, half stunned still, but wholly sobered. He tried to shake them off, but they answered that he must first apologise to his Grace. He refused, and they threatened him with the pond. He gave in then, in a way, speaking one thing, but looking another, which was yet the plainer of the two to the Duke. It meant that all was not yet over between him and Hunt. And

Jack was very silent as he led Olivia back to the terrace.

"You were quite right," she said as they went; "had I been a man I would have done it for you."

"You're a splendid girl," he replied, to her confusion; but that was all; nor did he seem conscious of what he said.

Already it was late, and in another hour the band had stopped; the fireworks were over; the people all gone, and gone the memory of their ringing cheers from the heart of the Duke, who stood alone with Claude Lafont on the moonlit terrace. Claude had heard of Hunt's insolence and summary chastisement; he regretted the incident extremely; but his state of mind was nothing to that of the Duke, who was now a prey to reactionary depression of the severest order.

"Are there any revolvers in the house?" said he. "I shall want a loaded one to-night."

"What in the world for?" cried Claude in dismay.

"Not for my own brains; you needn't alarm yourself. But you see what a bitter enemy I've made; he might get me at his mercy out there at the hut. There was murder in his eye to-night, or else truth in his words, and that you

won't allow. But there was one or the other.
So I want a shooter before I go over."

"If only you wouldn't go over at all! What's
the use, when there are dozens of good rooms
lying idle in the house? It does seem a madness!"

"Well, I am half thinking of giving it up;
but not to-night, or that brute may go killing
my cats. ˙ He's capable of anything. Give me
a revolver like a good chap."

Claude fetched one from the gun-room. He
it was who still knew the whereabouts of all
things, who kept the keys, and who arranged
most matters for the Duke. He was Jack's
major-domo as well as his guide, philosopher,
and friend.

To-night they walked together as far as the
shores of the lake. Claude then returned, but
for some reason the pair shook hands first. No
word was said, save between eye and eye in the
pale light of the new harvest moon. But Claude
had never yet seen his cousin gaze so kindly on
the home of their common ancestors as he did
to-night before they separated. And that look
was a consolation to the poet as he returned
alone to the house.

"This is the last link with that miserable
bush life," said Claude to himself; "and it's

very nearly worn through. He's beginning to see that there wasn't so much after all in the inheritance of Esau. After to-night we shall have no more of this nonsense of camping out in a make-believe bush hut; he will sleep under his own roof, like a sane man, and I'll get him to burn the bush hut down. After that — after that — well, I suppose the wedding-bells and the altar rails are only a question of time!"

And Claude went within, to talk of art and of books until bookman and artist went to bed; but he himself returned to the terrace instead of following their example. A dark depression was brooding over his spirit, his mind was full of vague forebodings. He had also a hundred regrets, and yet the last and the least of these was for the moment the most poignant too. He was sorry he had yielded to Jack in the matter of that revolver. And even as the thought came into his head — by some strange prescience — surely never by coincidence — he heard a shot far away in the direction of the lake. He held his breath, and heard a single throb of his own heart; then another shot; and then another and another until he had counted five.

Now it was a five-chambered revolver that Claude had handed fully loaded to his cousin.

CHAPTER XII

THE WRONG MAN

THE Duke had proceeded to his hut with the slow and slouching gait of a man bemused; yet the strings of his body were as those of a lute, and there was an inordinate keen edge to his every sense. He heard the deer cropping the grass far behind him; and he counted the very reverberations of the stable clock striking a half-hour in the still air. It was the half-hour after midnight. The moon still slanted among the pines, and Jack followed his own shadow, with his beard splayed against his shirt-front, until within a few yards of his hut. Then he looked quickly up and about. But the hut was obviously intact; there was the moon twinkling in the padlock of which the key was in his pocket; and Jack returned to his examination of the ground.

He was a very old bushman; he had a black-fellow's eye for a footprint, and he had struck a trail here which he knew to be recent and not his own. He followed it to the padlocked door, and round the hut and back to the door. He found the two heel-marks where the man had sat down to think some matter over. Then he took out his key and went within, but left the door wide open; and while his back was still turned to it, for he could not find his matches, there was a slight noise there, and the moon's influx was stemmed by a man's body.

"Good morning, Hunt," said Jack, without turning round.

The tone, no less than the words, took the intruder all aback. He had planned a pretty surprise, only to receive a prettier for his pains.

"How did you know it was me?" he cried.

"By your voice," was the reply; and the matches were found at last.

"But before that?"

"I expected you. Why didn't you go on sitting there with your back to the door?"

"You saw me!" cried Hunt, coming in.

"I saw your tracks. Hullo! Be good enough to step outside again."

"I've come to talk to you——"

"Quite so; but we'll talk outside."

And Hunt had to go with what grace he might. Jack followed with a couple of camp-stools, pulled the door to, sat down on one of the stools, and motioned Hunt to the other. The great smooth face shook slowly in reply; and the moonlight showed a bulbous bruise between the eyes, which made its author frown and feel at fault.

"Yes, you may look!" said Hunt through the gap in his set teeth which was a piece of the same handiwork. "You hit hard enough, but I can hit harder where it hurts more. A fine Duke *you* are! Oh, yes; double your fists again — do. You won't hit me this time. There's no one looking on!"

"Don't be too sure, my boy," replied Jack. "Don't you make any mistake!"

Hunt stuck a foot upon his camp-stool and leant forward over his knee.

"Recollect why you struck me to-night?"

"Perfectly."

"Well, I deserved it — for being such a fool as to say what I had to say at a time like that. It was the drink said it, not me; I apologise again for saying it there, I apologise to you and me too. I was keeping it to say here."

"Out with it," said Jack, who to his own astonishment was preserving a perfect calm; as he spoke he began filling a pipe that he had brought out with the matches.

"One thing at a time," said Hunt, producing

a greasy bank-book. "I'll out with this first. You may have heard that the old Duke had a kind of weakness for my folks?"

"I have heard something of the sort."

"Then I'll trouble you to run your eye over this here pass-book. It belongs to my old dad. It'll show you his account with the London and Provincial Bank at Devenholme. It's a small account. This here book goes back over ten years, and there's some blank leaves yet. But look at it for yourself; keep your eye on the left-hand page from first to last; and you'll see what you'll see."

Jack did so; and what he saw on every left-hand page was this: "per Maitland, £50." There were other entries, "by cheque" and "by cash," but they were few and small. Clearly Maitland was the backbone of the account; and a closer inspection revealed the further fact that his name appeared punctually every quarter, and always in connection with the sum of fifty pounds received.

"Ever heard of Maitland, Hollis, Cripps and Co.?" inquired Hunt.

Jack started; so this was the Maitland. "They are my solicitors," he said.

"They were the old Duke's too," replied Hunt. "Now have a look at the other side of the account. You know the Lower Farm; then look and see what we pay for rent."

"I know the figure," said Jack, handing back the pass-book. "It is half the value."

"Less than half — though I say it! And what does all this mean — two hundred a year paid up without fail by Maitland, Hollis, Cripps and Co., and the Lower Farm very near rent free? It means," said Hunt, leaning forward, with an evil gleam on either side of his angry bruise — "it means that something's bought of us as doesn't appear. You can guess what for yourself. Our silence! Two hundred a year, and the Lower Farm at a nominal rent, all for keeping a solitary secret!"

"Then I should advise you to go on keeping it," said Jack, with cool point; yet for all his nonchalance, his heart was in a flutter enough now; for he knew what was coming — he caught himself wondering how much or how little it surprised him.

"All very fine," he heard Hunt saying — a long way off as it seemed to him — whereas he was really bending farther forward than before. "All very fine! But what if this secret has improved in value with keeping? Improved, did I say? Lord's truth, it's gone up a thousand per cent. in the last few weeks; and who do you suppose sent it up? Why, you! I'll tell you how. I dessay you can guess; still I'll tell you, then there'll be no mistakes. You've heard things of your father? You know the sort he was? You won't knock me down again for mentioning it, will you? I thought not! Well, when the Red Marquis, as they used to call him, was a young man about the house here, my old dad was in the stables; and my old dad's young sister was the Duchess's own maid — a slapping fine girl, they tell me, but she was dead before I can remember. Well, and something happened; something often does. But this was something choice. Guess what!"

"He married her."

"He did. He married her at the parish church of Chelsea, in the name of Augustus William Greville Maske, his real name all but the title; still, he married the girl."

"Quite right too!"

"Oh, quite right, was it? Stop a bit. You were born in 1855. You told me so yourself; you may remember the time, and you stake your life *I* don't forget it. It was the sweetest music I ever heard, was that there date! Shall I tell you why? Why, because them two — the Red Marquis and his mother's maid — were married on October 22d, 1853."

“Well?”

Hunt took out a handful of cigars which had been provided for all comers in the evening; he had filled his pockets with them; and now he selected one by the light of the setting moon and lit it deliberately. Then he puffed a mouthful of smoke in Jack’s direction, and grinned.

“‘Well,’ says you; and you may well ‘well!’ For the Red Marquis deserted his wife and went out to Australia before he’d been married a month. And out there he married again. *But you were five years old, my fine fellow, before his first wife died, and was buried in this here parish!* You can look at her tombstone for yourself. She died and was buried as Eliza Hunt; and just that much was worth two hundred a year to us for good and all; because, you see, I’m sorry to say she never had a child.”

Both in substance and in tone this last statement was the most convincing of all. Here was an insolent exultation tempered by a still more insolent regret; and the very incompleteness of the triumph engraved it the deeper with the stamp of harsh reality.

Jack saw his position steadily in all its bearings. He was nobody. A little time ago he had stepped into Claude’s shoes, but now Claude would step into his. Well, thank God that it was Claude!   And yet — and yet — that saving fact made facts of all the rest.

"I've no doubt your yarn is quite true," said Jack, still in a tone that amazed himself.   "But of course you have some proofs on paper?"

"Plenty."

"Then why couldn't you come out with all this before?"

Hunt gave so broad a grin that a volume of smoke escaped haphazard from his gaping mouth.

"You'd punished me," he said, admiring the red end of his cigar; "I'd got you to punish in your turn, and with interest.   So I gave you time to get to like the old country in general, and this here spot in particular; to say nothing of coming the Duke; I meant that to grow on you too.   I hope as I gave you time enough? This here hut don't look altogether like it, you know!"

Jack's right hand was caressing the loaded revolver in the breast-pocket of his dress-coat; it was the cold, solid power of the little living weapon that kept the man himself cool and strong in his extremity.

"Quite fair," he remarked.   "Any other reason?"

"One other."

"What was that?"

"Well, you see, it's like this" — and Hunt dropped his insolence for a confidential tone far harder to brook. "It's like this," he repeated, plumping down on the camp-stool in front of Jack: "there's nobody knows of that there marriage but us Hunts. We've kep' it a dead secret for nearly forty years, and we don't want to let it out now. But, as I say, the secret's gone up in value. Surely it's worth more than two hundred a year to you? You don't want to be knocked sideways by that there Claude Lafont, do you? Yet he's the next man. You'd never let yourself be chucked out by a chap like that?"

"That's my business. What's your price?"

"Two thousand."

"A year?"

"Two thousand a year. Come, it's worth that to you if it's worth a penny-piece. Think of your income!"

"Think of yours. Two hundred on condition you kept a single secret! That was the condition, wasn't it?"

"Well?"

"You've let the secret out, you cur!" cried Jack, jumping to his feet. "And you've lost your income by it for good and all. Two thousand! You'll never see another two hundred.

What, did you take me for a dirty skunk like yourself? Do you think I got in this position through my own fault or of my own accord? Do you think I'm so sweet on it as to sit tight at the mercy of a thing like you? Not me! What you've told me to-night the real Duke and his lawyers shall hear to-morrow; and think yourself lucky if you aren't run in for your shot at a damnable conspiracy! Did you really suppose I cared as much as all that? Do you think — oh! for God's sake, clear out, man, before I do you any more damage!"

"Oh, you're good at that," said Hunt through his broken tooth. He had risen, and now he retreated a few paces. "You're not bad with your fists, you fool, but I've come prepared for you this time!" and he drew a knife; but the revolver covered him next instant.

"And I for you," retorted Jack. "I give you five seconds to clear out in. One — two — "

"My God, are there such fools — "

"Three — four — "

The man was gone. At a safer range he stopped again to threaten and gloat, to curse and to coax alternately. But Jack took no more notice; he turned into the hut, flung the pistol on the table, and stood motionless until the railing died away. Yet he had heeded never a word of it, but was rather reminded that it had been by its very cessation, as one notes the stopping of a clock. It made him look out once more, however; and, looking, he saw the last of Matthew Hunt in the moonlit spaces among the pines. His retreating steps died slowly away. The snapping of a twig was just audible a little after. And then in the mellow distance the stable clock chimed and struck one; and again Jack found himself keeping an imaginary count of the reverberations until all was still.

He stood at the door a moment longer. The feathered barbs of the pine-trees were drawn in ink upon a starry slate. The night was as mild and clear and silent as many a one in the Riverina itself; and Jack tried to think himself there; to regard this English summer as the bushman's dream that he had so often imagined it here in his model bush hut. But his imagination was very stubborn to-night. The stately home which was not his rose in his mind's eye between him and the stars; once more he saw it illumined in a flash from spire to terrace; once more the portico columns marched forward as one man, while the six eagles flew out in the tympanum above; and though a purring arose from his feet, and something soft and warm rubbed kindly against his shins, he could no longer forget where he was and who he was not. He was not the Duke. He was the wrong man after all. And the hut that he had built and inhabited, as a protest against all this grandeur, was a monument of irony such as the hand of man had never reared in all the world before.

The wrong man! He flung himself upon the elaborately rude bed to grapple with those three words until he might grasp what they meant to himself. And as he lay, his little cat leapt softly up and purred upon his heart, as if it knew the aching need there of a sympathy beyond the reach of words.

Only one aspect of his case came home to him now, but that was its worst aspect. The life he was to lose mattered little after all. He might miss it more than he had once thought; it was probable he would but truly appreciate it when it was a life of the past, as is the way of a man. Yet even that could be borne. The losing of the girl was different and a million times worse. But lose her he must: for what was he now? Instead of a Duke a nobody; not even a decently born peasant; a nameless husk of humanity, a derelict, a nonentity, the natural son of a notorious rake. Must he go back then to the bush, and back alone? Must he put himself beyond the reach of soft words and softer eyes for ever? He could feel again that little hand within his arm; and it was worse a hundred-fold than the vision of the Towers lit from end to end by the light of a bursting rocket. Would not the grave itself——

Wait.

There was the pistol on the table. The pale light lay along the barrel. He held his breath and lay gazing at the faint gleam until it grew into a blinding sun that scorched him to the soul. And he hardly knew what he had done when Claude Lafont found him wandering outside with the hot pistol still in his hand.

Jack looked upon the breathless poet with dull eyes that slowly brightened; then he pressed the lever, shot out the empty cartridges, blew through the chambers, and handed the revolver back to Claude.

"I've no more use for it. I'm much obliged to you. No, I've done no damage with it; that's just the point. I was emptying it for safety's sake. I'm so sorry you heard. I—I *did* think of emptying it—through my own head."

"In Heaven's name, why?"

"Only for a moment, though. It would have

been a poor trick after all. Still I had to empty it first and see that afterwards."

"But why? What on earth has happened?"

"I'm not the man after all."

"What man?"

"The Duke of St. Osmund's."

And Claude was made to hear everything before he was allowed the free expression of his astonishment and incredulity. Then he laughed. His incredulity remained.

"My dear fellow," he cried, "there's not a word of truth in the whole story. It's one colossal fraud. Hunt's a blackguard. I wouldn't believe his oath in a court of justice."

"What about the bank-book?"

"A fraud within a fraud!"

"Not it. I'll answer for that. Oh, no; we could have inquired at the bank. Hunt's a blackguard, but no fool. And you know what my father was; from all accounts he wasn't the man to think twice about a little job like bigamy."

"I wouldn't say that; few men of our sort would be so reckless in such a matter," declared the poet. "Now, from all *I* know of him, I should have said it was most inconsistent with his character to marry the girl at all. Everything but that! And surely it's quite possible to explain even that two hundred a year without swallowing such a camel as downright bigamy. My grandfather was a sort of puritanical monomaniac; even in the days of his mental vigour I can remember him as a sterner moralist than any of one's school-masters or college dons. Then, too, he was morbidly sensitive about the family failings and traditions, and painfully anxious to improve the tone of our house. Bear that in mind and conceive as gross a scandal as you like — but not bigamy. Do you mean to tell me that a man like my grandfather would have thought two hundred a year for all time too much to pay for hushing such a thing up for all time? Not he — not he!"

There fell a heavy hand upon Claude's back.

"Claude, old boy, I always said you were a genius. Do you know, I never thought of that?"

"It's obvious; besides, there's the Eliza Hunt on the gravestone, I've seen it myself. But look here — I'll tell you what I'll do."

"What, old man?"

"I'll run up to town to-morrow and see Maitland, Hollis, Cripps about the whole matter. They've paid the money; they are the men to know all about it. Stop a moment! Hunt was clever enough to have an exact date for the marriage. What was it again?"

"October 22d, 1853."

"I think he said Chelsea *parish* church?"

"He did."

Claude scribbled a note of each point on his shirt-cuff.

"That's all I want," said he. "I'll run up by the first train, and back by the last. Meanwhile, take my word for it, you're as safe as the Queen upon her throne."

"And you?" said Jack.

"Oh, never mind me; I'm very well as I am."

Claude was fully conscious of his semi-heroic attitude; indeed he enjoyed it, as he had enjoyed many a less inevitable pose in his day. But that he could not help; and Jack was perhaps the last person in the world to probe beneath the surface of a kind action. His great hand found Claude's, and his deep voice quivered with emotion.

"I don't know how it is," he faltered, "but this thing has got at me more than I meant it to. Hark at that! Three o'clock; it'll be light before we know where we are; you won't leave a fellow till it is, will you? I'm in a funk! I've got to believe the worst till I know otherwise — that's all about it. The day I shan't mind tackling by myself, but for God's sake don't go and leave me to-night. You've got to go in the morning ; stop the rest of the night out here with me. You shall have the bunk, and I'll doss down on the floor. I'll light the fire and brew a billy of tea this minute if only you'll stay with me now. Didn't you once say you'd have hold of my sleeve? And so you have had, old man, so you have had : only now's your time — more than ever."

Claude was deeply moved by the spectacle of a stronger man than himself so stricken in every nerve. He looked very compassionately upon the eager open face. There were a few grey hairs about either temple, but in the faint starlight they looked perfectly white; and there were crow's-feet under the eyes that seemed to have escaped his attention till now. He consented to remain on one condition: he must go back and put out the lights, and close the windows in the Poet's Corner. So Jack went with him; and those lights were the only sign of life in all the vast expanse of ancient masonry, that still belonged to one of them, though they knew not now to which. It was this thought, perhaps, that kept both men silent on the terrace when the lights had been put out and the windows shut. Then Jack ran his arm affectionately through that of Claude, and together they turned their backs upon those debatable stones.

CHAPTER XIII

THE INTERREGNUM

LADY CAROLINE SELLWOOD was delighted to
find Jack in the hall on making her descent
next morning. He appeared lost, however, in
a gloomy admiration of the ghostly guard in
armour. The attitude and the expression were
alike so foreign to him that Lady Caroline
halted on the stairs. But only for a moment;
the next, Jack was overwhelmed by the soft
tempest of her goodwill, and making prodigious
efforts to return her smiles.

Suddenly she became severe.

"You're knocked up! You look as if you
hadn't had a wink of sleep. Oh, I knew how it
would be after all that racket; you dear, naughty
Duke, you should have spared yourself more!"

I was a fool," admitted Jack. "But — but
I say, Lady Caroline, I do wish you wouldn't
Duke me!"

"How sweet of you," murmured Lady Caroline.

“ You know you didn’t last night! ” he
hastily reminded her.

“ But that was an occasion.”

“ So is this ! ” exclaimed Jack, and his tone
struck the other more than she showed.

“ Where is Claude? ” inquired Lady Caroline
suddenly.

“ On his way to Devenholme.”

“ Devenholme ! ”

“ And London, for the day. He had to catch
the 9.40.”

“ So he has gone up to town ! Odd that one
never heard anything about it — I mean to say
he could have made himself so useful to one.
May I ask when he decided to go? ”

Jack hesitated. He had been charged to keep
a discreet tongue during Claude’s absence; he
had been supplied with a number of reasons and
excuses ready-made; but perfect frankness was
an instinctive need of this primitive soul, whose
present thoughts stood out in easy print upon
his face, even as he resolved to resist his instincts for once.

“ He decided — this morning,” said Jack at
last; and he took from his pocket a lengthy
newspaper cutting attached to a pale green slip:
“ This is an article on him and his books, that
has just appeared in the *Parthenon*. What

wouldn't I give to lay a hold of the brute who wrote it! I call it the sort of thing to answer with a hiding. It's one of a series headed 'Our Minor Poets,' which Claude says has been bad enough all through; but this article on him is the worst and most brutal of the lot. And— and—and old Claude took it to heart, of course; and — and he's run up to town for the day."

"Because of a severe criticism! I should have thought he was used to them by now. Poor dear Claude, he can string a pretty rhyme, but he never was a poet. And you, Jack— since you insist— you never were an actor— until to-day!"

Jack hung his head.

"You don't do it well enough, you dear fellow," continued Lady Caroline caressingly. "As if you could impose upon me! You must first come to me for lessons. Candidly now: what has taken him up to town in such a hurry? The same thing that—kept you awake all night?"

"Candidly, then," said Jack, raising his haggard face doggedly, "it was! And if you'll come out upon the terrace for five minutes I'll tell you exactly what's wrong. You have a right to know; and I can trust *you* not to let it go any further for the moment. Even if I couldn't,

I’d have to tell you straight! I hate keeping
things up my sleeve; I can’t do it; so let me
make a clean breast of the whole shoot, Lady
Caroline, and be done with it till Claude comes
back.”

Lady Caroline took a discouraging view of
the situation. The Red Marquis had been capable of anything; related though they had been,
she could not help telling Jack that her parents
had forbidden her to dance with his father as a
young girl. This might be painful hearing, but
in such a crisis it was necessary to face the
possibilities; and Lady Caroline, drawing a little
away from her companion in order to see how
he was facing them, forgot to take his arm any
more as they sauntered in the sun. She under-
took, however, to keep the matter to herself
until Claude’s return, at the mention of whose
name she begged to look at the cutting from
the *Parthenon.*

“A most repulsive article,” her mother informed Olivia after breakfast, but not until she
had repeated to the girl the entire substance of
the late conversation on the terrace. “I never
read anything more venomously ill-bred in my
life; and so untrue! To say he is no poet —
our Claude! But we who know him, thank
goodness we know better. It is the true poetry,

not only in but between every line, that distinguishes dear Claude from the mere stringers of pretty rhymes of whom the papers sicken one in these latter days. But where are you going, my love?"

"To get ready to go with — Jack."

"To go where, pray?"

"Why, to Devenholme, as we arranged last night," replied Olivia, with spirit. "He said he would drive me over; and *you* said 'how sweet of him,' and beamed upon us both!"

Lady Caroline winced. "You impertinent chit!" she cried viciously; "you know as well as I do that what I have told you alters everything. Once and for all, Olivia, I forbid you to drive into Devenholme with — with — with — that common man!"

"Very well; the drive's off," said the girl with swift decision; and she left her mother without another word.

She put on her habit and went straight to Jack.

"Do you mind if we *ride* into Devenholme instead of driving?"

"Mind! I should like it even better."

"Then suppose we go to the stable-yard and see about our horses ourselves; and while we are there, we may as well stay and start by the back road, which will save at least a quarter of a mile.”

“My oath,” said Jack without further provocation, “you might have been dragged up in the bush!”

“I wish I had been!” exclaimed Olivia bitterly. He could not understand her tone. Nor did he ever know the meaning of the momentary fighting glitter in the brave brown eyes of the girl.

He rode as an inveterate bushman, entirely on the snaffle, with inelegantly short stirrups and a regrettable example of the back-block bend; nor did his well-broken hack give him a chance of exhibiting any of the finer qualities of the rough-riding school. But indeed for the most part the couple sat at ease in their saddles, while the horses dawdled with loose reins and lazy necks in the cool shadows of the roadside trees. By mutual consent they had dispensed with an attendant groom. And Olivia had never been so kind to Jack, as on this day when he was under so black a cloud, with so heavy a seal upon his lips.

For once she talked to him; as a rule she liked better to listen, with large eyes intent and sympathetic lips apart — ever ready with the helpful word. But to-day she was wishful to

entertain, to take him out of himself, to console
without letting him suspect that she knew as
much as he had told her mother. In a sense
she knew more, for Lady Caroline had duly
exaggerated his frank confession; and the girl's
heart bled for her friend, on the brink of a
disillusion without parallel in her knowledge.
So she told him of her life in town and elsewhere; of the treadmill round of toilsome pleasure; of the penance of dressing and smiling
with unflagging prettiness; of the hollow friend-
ships and hollower loves of that garish life, and
the unutterable staleness of the whole conventional routine. No doubt she overstated her
case; and certainly her strictures were themselves conventional; but she was perfectly aware
of both facts, and would have been exceedingly
sorry to have had this conversation recorded
against her. Olivia had a healthy horror of
superiority, either of the moral or the intellectual order. But she was conducting a conversation with an obvious purpose; and it was
only when he told her again, and more earnestly
than before, how suited she was for the bush,
that she proposed the canter which brought
them a mile nearer Devenholme.

"Now it's you to play," she told him as they
drew rein; "and I want to hear some of your

adventures. You've never told us any, yet you must have had heaps. So far I've only heard about the hut, the sheep, the homestead, and your old boss."

"A white man!" cried Jack. "I wish you knew him."

"So do I; but I can quite picture him, and just now I would much rather hear about some of your own adventures. So begin."

Jack laughed.

"Really, Miss Sellwood, I never had one in my life!"

"Then really, my Lord Duke, I can't believe a word ——"

Jack was laughing no more.

"Don't call me that," he said. "It would be so much kinder to call me Jack!"

She had forgotten. Her heart smote her now, and the difficulty was to conceal her unsuspected sympathy. So she insisted on his calling her Olivia, to conclude the bargain. And the double innovation made them both so self-conscious, that she forgot her thirst for his adventures, while he brooded heavily upon his bitter-sweet advancement won too late.

So they came into Devenholme as the sun was shining fore and aft along the quaint old English streets. And in the town, where he was well enough known by this time, poor Jack was received with a cruel consideration that would have hurt him even more than it did had he dreamt how it affected his companion. The tender-hearted girl was inexpressibly grieved, and never more than when the jeweller mentioned a hundred guineas as the price of the ring to be changed; indeed, the situation in the jeweller's shop was perilously charged with hidden emotions. In this terribly equivocal position, Jack could not press upon Olivia things for which he might never be able to pay; neither could Olivia now refuse any present at all, nor yet lead him as low as she would have liked in the price, for fear of revealing her illicit knowledge. So at last they hit upon a curb-bracelet that fastened with a tiny padlock. It cost but forty-five shillings. And when he had locked it upon her right wrist, he pocketed the key without a remark, then paid ready money and left the shop in a throbbing agony of shame. The poor jeweller stood bowing them out with the hundred-guinea ring still in his hand.

CHAPTER XIV

JACK AND HIS MASTER

IT · was necessary to bait the horses; it was
equally essential for the pair themselves to have
something to eat. So they rode under the olden
arch of the oak-lined Falcon, and it was "your
Grace" at every step, with ironic iteration very
hard for either of them to bear without a word
to the other. They dismounted therefore with
the less delay; and Olivia turned her back upon
the coffee-room window, and on an elderly, bald,
well-dressed man, whose cool fixed stare made
the girl extremely angry, when Jack at her side
gave a shout of delight.

"So help me never! *it's the boss himself!*"

Olivia turned, and there was the objectionable
old fellow in the window smiling and waving
to her enchanted companion. And this was the
man of whom she had heard so often! She did
not stop to consider how he came to be here; the
back-blockers were already at explanations, but
Olivia was not listening. She was thinking of

the bearded, jovial, hearty squatter of her imagination; and she was glancing askance at the massive chin and forehead, and at the white moustache cropped close over the bad mouth of the real man.

"Mr. Dalrymple — my old boss — Miss Sellwood!" shouted Jack, introducing them with a wealth of pantomime. "We're coming up to lunch with you, sir; that is, you're to lunch with me; it's my shout!"

And poor Olivia found herself swept off her feet, as it were, into the presence of a man whom all her instincts had pronounced odious at sight.

But the higher court of the girl's intellect reversed this judgment on the appeal of her trained perceptions. The elderly squatter was not after all a man to be summed up at a glance or in a word: his undoubted assurance was tempered and redeemed by so many graces of manner and address as to upset entirely the girl's preconceptions of his class. At table he treated her with a princely courtesy, imperceptibly including her in a conversation which poor Jack would have conducted very differently if left to himself. After the first few minutes, indeed, Olivia could see but two faults in the squatter; the first was the fierce light his charming manners reflected on those of Jack; and the second was a mouth which made the girl regret the austere cut of his moustache whenever she looked at Mr. Dalrymple.

"So you left before shearing, sir!" cried Jack, who was grossly eager for all station news. "I wonder you did that. They must be in the thick of it now!"

"They were to begin on the fifth of this month. The shearing, Miss Sellwood, is the one divine, far-off event towards which the whole sheep-station moves," added Mr. Dalrymple, with a glibness worthy of Claude Lafont.

"And don't you forget the lamb-marking," chimed in Jack. "I hope it was a good lambing this year, sir?"

"Seventy-nine per cent.," replied Dalrymple. "I'm afraid that's Greek to you, Miss Sellwood —and perhaps better so."

"You see, I'm as keen as ever on the old blocks!" cried Jack. It was a superfluous boast.

"So I do see; and I must say, Jack, you surprise me. Do you notice how he 'sirs' me, Miss Sellwood? I was on my way to pay homage to the Duke of St. Osmund's, not to receive it from Happy Jack of Carara!"

"Do you often come over to England, Mr.

Dalrymple?" asked Olivia quickly. For the girl had seen the spasm in Jack's face, and she knew how the anæsthetic of this happy encounter had exhaled with the squatter's last speech.

"No, indeed!" was the reply. "I haven't been home for more years than I care to count; and the chances are that I shouldn't be here now but for our friend the Duke. He unsettled me. You see, Miss Sellwood, how jealous are the hearts of men! *I* had no inheritance to come home to; but I had my native land, and here I am."

"And you have friends in Devenholme?"

"I have one friend; I wish that I dared say two," replied the squatter, looking from Jack to Olivia in his most engaging manner. "No, to tell you frankly, I was on a little inquisitive pilgrimage to Maske Towers. I did not wait for an invitation, for I knew that I should bring my own welcome with me."

"Of course, of course; come out to-morrow!" exclaimed Jack nervously. "I'll send in for you, and you must stay as long as ever you can. If only I'd driven in, as I meant to, we'd have taken you back with us. Yet on the whole to-morrow will be best; you must give us time to do you well, you know, Mr. Dalrymple. It'll

be a proud day for me! I little expected to
live to entertain my own boss!"

Indeed, his pride was genuine enough, and
truly characteristic of the man; but at the back
of it there was a great uneasiness which did not
escape the clear, light eye of Dalrymple. Not
that the squatter betrayed his prescience by
word or sign; on the contrary, he drank Jack's
health in the champagne provided by him, and
included Olivia's name in a very graceful speech.
But Jack drank nothing at all; and having reduced his roll to a heap of crumbs, he was now
employed in converting the crumbs into a pile
of pellets.

Olivia pitied his condition; that tremulous
brown hand, with the great bush freckles still
showing at the gnarled finger-roots, touched her
inexpressibly as it lay fidgeting on the white
table-cloth. She strained every nerve to keep
the squatter engaged and unobservant; and she
found herself fluctuating, in a rather irritating
manner, between her first instinctive antipathy
and her later liking for the man. He was extremely nice to her; he had an obvious kindness for poor Jack; and she apprehended a
personal magnetism, a unique individuality,
quite powerful enough to account for Jack's
devotion to him. She felt the influence herself.

Yet there was something — she could not say what.

The way in which her last vague prejudice was removed, however, made a deep impression upon Olivia, besides giving her a startling glimpse of her own feelings. And it all came of a casual remark of Dalrymple's, in elucidation of his prompt expedition to the district, to the effect that the Duke of St. Osmund's had once saved his life.

"Your life!" cried Olivia, while Jack ceased meddling with his bread.

"To be sure. Is it possible he has never told you the story?"

"Not a word of it! And only this morning, as we rode in, I asked him if he had never had any adventures!"

Her face was a flushed reproach.

"I'd forgotten that one," said Jack sheepishly. "I really had. It's so long ago; and it wasn't much when you come ——"

"Not much!" interjected Dalrymple. "I should be very sorry to find myself in such a tight place again! It's some thirteen years ago, Miss Sellwood. I was thinking of taking up some cattle country in the unfenced part of Queensland. I had gone up to have a look at the place, and the blacks attacked us while I was there. We were three strong in an iron store: the owner, a stray shearer, and myself. The shearer had his horse hung up outside; he could have got away quite easily in the beginning; but our horses were all turned out, and he wouldn't leave us. So we dragged his horse inside, and we set to work to defend the store."

" I know that shearer!" cried Olivia proudly. "Yet he hangs his head! Oh, go on, Mr. Dalrymple, go on!"

" From daybreak to sundown," continued the squatter, "we defended ourselves with a Winchester, a double-barrelled shot-gun, and an old muzzle-loading rifle. The blacks came on by the score, but they couldn't get in, and they couldn't set fire to the corrugated iron. It was riddled like a sieve, and each of us three had a hole in him too; but there was a wall of dead blacks up against the iron outside, and they were as good as sandbags. We should have beaten the fellows off before midnight if our powder had held out. It didn't; so I assure you we shook hands, and were going to blow up the place with a twenty-gallon tin of petroleum, that was luckily inside, when our friend the shearer came out with an idea. His horse had a ball in its body and was screaming like a woman, so that *it* was no use. I recollect we put it out of its pain with our last charge.   But there was long dry grass all round up to within some fifteen yards of the store; and after dark the shearer ran out three or four times with a bucket of petroleum, and once with a box of matches.   The last time but one the blacks saw him.   They had surrounded the place at a pretty respectful radius, and they were having what we call a spell; but they saw him the last time but one.   And when he went out again and struck his matches they had something to aim at. Well, his first match went out, and there was a sheaf of spears sticking in the sand and three new holes through the house.   We waited; not another thing could we see.   We didn't know whether he was dead or alive, and we heard the blacks starting to rush us.   But we also heard the scratch of a second match; in another instant the thing flared up like a circular lamp — and us in the middle of the burner!   The country was burnt black for miles all round, and we ourselves had a hot time of it, Miss Sellwood; but here are two of us, at all events, to tell the tale."

Olivia bowed to him; she could not speak. Then for a little she turned her wet eyes, wet with enthusiasm, upon the awkward hero of the tale.   And without more words the party broke up.

Jack was still remonstrating with Dalrymple when the girl rejoined them outside.

"Come now!" she said. "Was it true, or wasn't it?"

"More or less," admitted Jack.

"Was it true about the horse and the petroleum and the spears?"

He confessed that it was, but discredited his memory as a clumsy qualification. Olivia turned away from him, and said no more until she was in her saddle; then while Jack was mounting she rode up to the squatter.

"I am truly grateful to you, Mr. Dalrymple," she said; "and all the others will be as grateful as I am, and will look forward to your visit. But for you, we might all have gone on being entertained by a hero unawares. You must tell us more. Meanwhile I for one can thank you most heartily!"

And she leant over and frankly pressed his hand; but said very little all the long ride home. Jack assured her, however, that he had never thought of his wound for years, although he must have a bullet in him somewhere to that day; he also told her that the fight with the blacks had been the beginning of his connection with his old boss, whose service he had never left until the end. And for miles he spoke of no one else; he was so grateful to Olivia for liking his friend, and he had so many stories of Dalrymple to set as well as he could against that one of himself. So the ride drew to an end in the golden afternoon, with never a tender word between the pair, though his heart was as full as hers; but she could not speak; and the great seal lay yet upon his lips.

CHAPTER XV

Nobody was about when they dismounted, so Jack himself led the horses back to the stables, while Olivia gathered up her habit and scaled the steps. The stable clock struck five as the former was returning by way of the shrubbery; another seven hours, and Claude would come home with the news. For such an issue, it was still an eternity to wait. But Jack felt that the suspense would be easily endurable so long as he could have sight and speech of Olivia Sellwood; without her, even for these few minutes, it was hardly to be borne.

Yet this stage of his ordeal was made up of such minutes. He returned to desolate rooms. Olivia had disappeared; nor could he pitch upon a soul to tell him where she was. Door after door was thrown open in vain; each presented an empty void to his exacting eyes. He ran outside and stood listening on the terrace. And there, through an open upper window he heard a raised voice railing, which he could not but recognise as that of Lady Caroline. Her words were indistinguishable. But as Jack looked aloft for the window, one was passionately shut, and he neither heard nor saw any more.

The first persons he ultimately encountered were Mr. Sellwood and the agent. They had golf-clubs in their hands and wholesome sweat upon their brows. The agent treated Jack as usual; the Home Secretary did not. He stated that he had at last won a round; but his manner was singularly free from exultation; indeed, it was quite awkward, as though perfect cordiality had suddenly become a difficult matter, and he was ashamed to find it so. Certainly there had been no difficulty of the kind before. And Jack noted the change, but was too honourable himself to suspect the cause.

He next fell in with the Frekes. This excellent couple loved Jack for his goodness to their children, who were not universally popular. They now carried him off to tea in the nursery, where he stayed until it was time to dress for dinner. Jack liked the children; it was not his fault that they were so seldom in evidence. They were obviously spoilt; but Jack thought they were taken too seriously by all but their parents, who certainly did not take them seriously enough. So he had many a romp with the little outcasts, but never a wilder one than this after-noon, for the children took him out of himself. Their society, had he but known it, was even better for him in the circumstances than that of Olivia herself; it was almost as good as another meeting with Dalrymple of Carara. He rose at length from under his oppressors, dusty, dis-hevelled and perspiring, but for the moment as light-hearted as themselves. And there were the grave, sympathetic eyes of the parents rest-ing sadly upon him to recall his trouble. Why should they look sad or sympathetic? Every-body had changed towards him; this was the difference in the Frekes. Could they have di-vined the truth? No suspicion of a broken con-fidence entered his head; yet it was sufficiently puzzled as he dressed, with unusual care, to make a creditable last appearance at the head of the table which would prove never to have been his at all. He had quite made up his mind to that; he found it appreciably harder to reconcile himself to the keen disappointment which awaited him in the dining-room.

Olivia was not coming down.

"She has knocked herself up," explained Lady Caroline tersely. "So would any girl

—not an Australian — who rode so far on such a day. Your Grace might have known better!"

Jack stared at her like a wounded stag; then he uttered an abject apology, for which, however, he obtained no sort of a receipt. Lady Caroline had turned and was talking to some one else. But it was not this that cut him to the heart; it was her mode of addressing him, after their conversation of the early morning.

Later in the evening he remembered that railing voice and the shutting of the window upstairs; and with a burning indignation he divined, all at once, who it was that had been so spoken to, and why, with the true cause of Olivia's indisposition.

This was in the darkness of his hut, with Livingstone asleep in his lap. In another minute Jack was striding through the pines, on his way to the drawing-room for a few plain words with Lady Caroline Sellwood. He never had them. Lady Caroline was gone to bed. It was almost eleven; within an hour Claude would be back, and a moral certainty become an absolute fact. Hunt's tale was true. Had it been otherwise, Claude would have telegraphed. He had left, indeed, on the distinct understanding that he should do no such thing; his mission was to be kept a secret, and a telegram might excite suspicion; yet even so he would have sent one had all been well. Jack was sure of it; his exhausted spirit had surrendered utterly to an ineluctable despair.

In this humour he sought the Poet's Corner, and found its two *habitués* furtively chuckling over some newspaper. Their gaiety cut him to the quick. Yet he longed to enter into it.

"What's the joke?" he asked. "I want something to make me laugh!"

"This wouldn't," replied Edmund Stubbs. "It's not benign enough for you."

"It's only a piece of smart scribbling," explained Llewellyn, lighting a fresh cigarette with the stump of the last.

Jack was behind them; quite innocently he put his head between theirs and looked for himself. The paper was the *Parthenon*. There was but one article on the open page. It was headed —

OUR MINOR POETS.

XXVIII. MR. CLAUDE LAFONT.

"So that amuses you?" said Jack at last.

"Quite," said Llewellyn.

"You think it just, eh?"

"Oh, hang justice! It's awfully nice copy. That's all it has any right to be. Justice doesn't matter a hang; the *Parthenon's* not written for the virtuous shopkeeper; it isn't meant to appeal to the Nonconformist Conscience."

"Besides, the article *is* just," protested Stubbs. "We know what Lafont is, between ourselves; he's an excellent chap, but his poetry — save the mark! — would hardly impose on Clapham and Wandsworth. His manner's cheap enough, but his matter goes one cheaper; it's the sort of thing for which there should be no charge." Stubbs drained his glass.

Jack was blazing.

"I don't know what you mean by 'cheap,'" he cried; "but from reading that article, which I happen to have seen before, I should call it a jolly 'cheap' word. I don't set up to be a clever man. I only know what I like, and I like everything of Claude's that — that I can understand. But even if I didn't I should be sorry to go about saying so in his own house!"

"*His* own house!" exclaimed the Impressionist.

"We didn't know it was his," said Stubbs.

"What's mine is Claude's," replied Jack, colouring. "It was before I turned up, and it will be again when — whenever I peg out."

With that he was gone.

"Sounds suicidal," remarked Llewellyn.

"Or celibate," said Stubbs, replenishing his glass.

"Poor beast!" concluded the artist.

Here their host returned.

"I'm very sorry, you fellows," said he, with absurd humility. "I'm all off colour to-night, and I know I've made a rude ruffian of myself. Some of these days you'll understand; meantime will you forgive me?"

"*I* have nothing to forgive," replied Llewellyn.

"We'll say no more about it," said Stubbs.

And Jack shook hands with them both before leaving them for good; then he hurried through the length of the building to the great conservatory, where Stebbings was putting out the lights. The conservatory was at that extreme of the Towers which the dogcart would pass first. Here, too, was room and air for a man distraught. So Jack called out to Stebbings to leave the lights on longer.

"And light some more," he added suddenly. "Light up every lamp in the place! I shall stay here until Mr. Lafont returns."

"Yes, your Grace."

"Stebbings!"

" Your Grace ? "

" For God's sake don't call me that again ! I — I'm not used to it, Stebbings — any more than you're used to me," added Jack inconsequently ; and he fled into the grounds until the old man should be gone.

The night was very dark and heavy ; clouds obscured the moon, shedding a fine rain softly upon drive and terrace. Jack raised his face, and a grateful sprinkling cooled its fever. He longed for a far heavier fall, with the ancient longing of those prehistoric days when a grey sky and an honest wetting were the rarest joys in life. Could he indeed return to that rough routine after all these weeks of aristocratic ease ? The bushman might exchange his wideawake for a coronet, but could the peer go back to the bush ? Time must show. The only question was whether Hunt had lied or told the truth ; and the answer could not be much longer delayed. Already it was half-past eleven ; there was the clang creeping lazily through the night, round quarter of a mile of intervening wall, and half a hundred angles.

He would have gone down the drive to meet the dogcart ; but the night was too dark ; and beside him blazed the great conservatory like a palace of fire. He entered it again, and now he had it to himself; the statues among the tree-ferns were his only companions. But in his absence old Stebbings had placed a little table with brandy and soda-water set out upon it; even the butler had seen and pitied his condition.

The third quarter struck. The sound just carried to the conservatory, for now the rain was heavier, and the rattle overheard warred successfully against all other noises. The dog-cart might drive by without Jack's hearing it. The suspense was horrible, but a surprise would be more horrible still. He was becoming unstrung; why should he not tune himself up with the brandy? His voluntary teetotalism was too absurd; he had made no promise, taken no pledge, but only a private pride in his self-discipline as it had gone on from day to day. Not a drop had he touched since that afternoon at Dover so long, so long ago! As he reckoned up the time, the forgotten lust possessed him; it had been even so on Carara, when the periodical need of a cheque would first steal over his lonely spirit. He thought now of those occasions and their results; he knew himself of old; but he was no longer the same man — resistance would be ridiculous now. He took another look at the night; then he filled a wine-glass with raw brandy — raised it — and im-

pulsively dashed the whole upon the marble flags.
The brandy widened in a shallow amber flood;
the broken glass lay glittering under the lamps;
and in Jack's ears the patter of the rain (which
had never abated) broke out anew.

He could not account for his act; he did not
know it for the culmination of a highly nervous
condition induced by the twenty-four sleepless
hours of unrelieved suspense. It was neither
more nor less, and yet it enabled him to hold up
his head once more. And as he did so, there —
through the swimming crystal walls — between
a palm-tree and a Norfolk Island pine — were
the two red eyes of the dogcart dilating in the
dark.

The great moment had come, and it was not
so great after all. Jack's little outburst had left
him strangely calm. He went to the door and
hailed the dogcart in a loud, cheery voice. The
lamps stopped. Claude came within range of
those in the conservatory, and shook himself on
the steps. Then he entered, looking unusually
healthy, but dripping still.

" A brute of a night for you," said Jack apologetically. " Take off that coat, and have some
brandy. Mind where you go. I've had a spill."

This was the reaction. Claude understood.

" Then you don't want to hear the news? "

"I know it. I've known it for hours."

"That I can see you haven't. Listen to me. There was no English marriage. Give me your hand!"

It was limp and cold.

"You don't believe me!" said Claude severely.

Jack subsided in a chair.

"I can't," he whispered. "I can't."

"You soon will. I wish to goodness I'd taken you with me to-day. Now listen: there was some truth in Hunt's story, but more lies. The marriage was a lie. There never was a marriage. There was something rather worse at the time, but a good deal better now. My grandfather patched it up, exactly as I thought. He packed my uncle out to Australia, and he settled two hundred a year on the Hunts, on the single condition of 'perpetual silence as to the connection between the two families.' I've seen the covenant, and those are the very words. The condition has been broken after all these years. And the Hunts' income stops to-day."

Jack had roused himself a little; he was no longer apathetic, but neither was he yet convinced.

"It seems a lot of money to hush up so small a matter," he objected. "Are they sure there was no more in it than that?"

r

"Maitland and Cripps?   Perfectly sure; they've been paying that money for nearly forty years, and there's never been a hint at a marriage until now.   Certainly there's none in the settlement.   But to make assurance surer, young Maitland took a cab and drove off to see his father — who was a partner in '53, but has since retired — about the whole matter.   And I took another cab, and drove straight to the old parish church facing the river at Chelsea.   I found the clerk, and he showed me the marriage register, but there was no such marriage on that date (or any other) in *that* church ; so why in any?   One lie means dozens.   Surely you'll agree with me there?"

"I must; it's only the money that sticks with me.   It seems such a case of paying through the nose.   But what had old Maitland to say?"

"Everything," cried Claude.   "He remembered the whole business perfectly, and even saying to my grandfather much what you're saying to me now.   But I've told you the kind of man the old Duke was; he was a purist of the purists, besides being as proud as Lucifer, and a scandal so near home hit him, as you would say, in both eyes at once.   He considered he got good value for his money when he hushed it up. They showed me a letter in which he said as much. Young Maitland unearthed it after he had seen his father, and with it others of a later date, in which the Duke refused to revoke or even to curtail the allowance on the woman's death. That's all; but surely it's conclusive enough! Here we have a first-class firm of solicitors on the one hand, and a clumsy scoundrel on the other. Which do you believe? By the way, they're anxious to prosecute Hunt on all sorts of grounds if you'll let them."

"I won't."

"I think you ought to," said Claude.

"No, no; too much mud has been stirred up already; we'll let it rest for a bit."

"But surely you'll get rid of the Hunts after this?"

"I'll see."

Claude was disappointed; he had looked for a different reception of his news.

"Do you mean to say you're not convinced yet?" he cried.

"No," said Jack, "I'm quite satisfied now; you hem the thing in on every side. But I wish to goodness all this had never happened!"

"So do we all; but if there was a doubt, surely it was best to set it at rest? If I were you, I should feel as one does after a bad dream."

Jack was on his feet.

"My dear old mate," he cried, "and so I do! But I'm only half woke up; that's what's the matter with me, and you must give me time to pull myself together. You don't know what a day I've had; you never will know. And you — my meat's your poison, and yet you've been doing all this for me just as if it was the other way round; and not a word of thanks at the end of it. Claude — old man — forgive me! Thanks won't do. They're no good at all in a case like this. What can a fellow say? If it was you, you'd say plenty —— "

"I hope not," interrupted Claude, laughing. "Wait till you do me a good turn. You've done me many a one already, and I've never said a word."

But Jack would shake hands, and even Claude's face was shining with a tender light as a soft step fell upon the marble, and Lady Caroline Sellwood entered from the drawing-room. The door had been left open. But it was instantly evident that her Ladyship had not been eavesdropping, or at least not to any useful purpose; for she planted herself before the two men in obvious ignorance as to which was the man for her. She was still in the handsome dress that she had worn all the evening; and between her plump, white, glittering fingers she nursed the purple smoking-cap that had always been — and was still — intended for the Duke of St. Osmund's.

"It was no good," she cried tragically, looking from Claude to Jack and back again at Claude. "I simply couldn't go to bed until I knew. And now—and now I'm torn two ways; for pity's sake put me out of *one* misery."

"It's all up," said Jack deliberately. He owed Lady Caroline a grudge for the shrill scolding he had heard upstairs, and another for Olivia's absence from the dinner-table. He was also curious to see what Lady Caroline would do.

She sailed straight to Claude, holding the smoking-cap at arm's length.

"My dear, dear Claude! *How* I congratulate you! I find, after all, that the smoking-cap, which was originally intended ——"

"Dear Lady Caroline," interposed Claude hastily, "everything is as it was. Hunt's story is a complete fabrication; I'd no idea that you knew anything about it."

"I couldn't help telling Lady Caroline," said Jack. Lady Caroline turned upon him with hot suspicion.

"You said it was all ——"

He interrupted her.

"I was *going* to say that it was all up with Hunt. He loses two hundred a year for his pains."

"Is that possible?" cried her Ladyship.

"It's the case," said Claude; "so everything is as it was, and as it should be."

Lady Caroline exhibited no further trace of her discomfiture.

"I wish we hadn't all interrupted each other," she laughed. "*I* was about to remark that the smoking-cap, which was originally intended to have what one may term a frieze, as well as a dado, of gold lace, will look much better without the frieze, so there's really no more to do to it. Take it, my dear, dear Jack, and wear it sometimes for my sake. And forgive a mother for what one said about Olivia's ride. Claude, I shall make another cap for you; meanwhile, let me congratulate you — again — on your noble conduct of to-day. Ah, you neither of you congratulate me on mine! Yet I am a woman, and I've kept your joint secret — most religiously — from nine in the morning to this very hour!"

CHAPTER XVI

"LOVE THE GIFT"

HER answer was altogether astonishing; she leant back in the boat and looked him full in the face. A quick flush tinged her own, and the incomparable eyebrows were raised and arched; but underneath there was an honest tenderness which Olivia was not the girl to conceal.

"Was that your water-lilies?" said she; but this was not the astonishing speech. He had lured her afloat on impudently false pretences; she had a right to twit him with that.

"There are no water-lilies," he confessed; "at least, never mind them if there are. Oh, I was obliged to make some excuse! There was nowhere else where we could talk so well. I tell you again I have the cheek to love you! I can't help it; I've loved you ever since that day in London, and you've got to know it for good or bad. If it makes you very angry, I'll row you back this minute." He was resting on

his oars under cover of the little island; the
Towers were out of sight.

" Why in the world didn't you speak yesterday?" was Olivia's extraordinary reply.

" Yesterday?" faltered Jack.

" It was such a chance!"

" Not for me! My tongue was tied. Olivia,
I was under a frightful cloud yesterday! You
don't understand ——"

" What if I do? What if I did at the time?"

" I don't see how you could," said Jack.

" Instinctively," replied Olivia, to screen her
mother. " I knew something was wrong, and
I have since been told what. If only you had
spoken then!"

She dropped her eyes swiftly; the tear ran
down her cheek.

" But why? Why then, better than now?"

" Because *I* care, too," she whispered, so that
the words just travelled to his ear.

" Olivia! My — do you know what you've
said? Do you mean it?"

" Of course I care. I mean that much. You
are different from everybody else."

" Then ——"

" There must be no ' then.'"

" But you said you cared. Tell me — I don't
understand."

"I can never marry you," said Olivia, looking him once more in the face. And her eyes were dry.

"Why not, if it is true — that you care?"

"Because you are what you are — and I — oh! how can I say it even to you? I am so ashamed. I have been thrown at your head from the very first — no, I have no right to say that. How I hate everything I say! You must understand; I am sure you do. Well, in the beginning I couldn't bear to speak to you, because I knew — what was hoped — and I seemed to see and hear it in every look and word. It hurt me more than I ever can tell you. The same sort of thing had happened before, but I had never minded it then. I suppose all mothers are like that; it's natural enough, when you come to think, and I'm sure I never resented it before. I wouldn't have minded it in your case either; I wouldn't have minded anything if I hadn't —— "

The words would not come.

"Hadn't what?" he said.

"If I hadn't liked you — off my own bat!"

"But if you really do, my glorious girl, surely that fixes it? We have nothing to do with anybody else. What does it matter how they take it?"

"It matters to my pride."

“I don’t see where your pride comes in.”

“Of course you don’t; you are not behind the scenes. And I can’t make you see. I’m not going to give my own people away to that extent, not even to you. But—I can just picture my mother’s face if we went in this very minute and told her we were engaged! She would fall upon both our necks!”

“That wouldn’t matter,” said Jack stolidly. “That would be all right.”

“It would be dreadful—dreadful. I couldn’t bear it when I know that yesterday——”

She checked herself firmly.

“Well, what of yesterday?”

“It would have been quite a different thing.”

“What! if I’d spoken then?”

“I — think so.”

“You would have said——”

“I should have found out what your trouble was. You would have told me everything. And then — and then——”

He leant still further forward.

“If you had wanted me very much——”

“I *do* want you very much.”

“I should have found it easier to say ‘yes’” —the word was hardly audible—“than I ever shall now!”

“But why, Olivia? Tell me why!”

"You force it from me, word by word," complained the girl.

"Then let me see. I think I begin to see. You like me in myself almost well enough to marry me. Well, thank God for that much! But you don't want to marry the Duke of St. Osmund's, because you're mortally afraid of what people will say. You think they'll say you're doing it for the main chance. And so they will—and so they may! They wouldn't say it, and you wouldn't think it, of any other man in my position; no, it's because I'm not fit for my billet, that's how it is! Not fit for it, and not fit for you; so they'd naturally think you were marrying me for what I'd got, and that you couldn't bear. Ah, yes, I see hard enough; it's as plain as a pikestaff now!"

The girl saw, too; with the unconscious bluntness of a singularly direct nature, he had stripped her scruples bare, and their littleness horrified Olivia. The moral cowardice of her hesitation came home to her with an insupportable pang, and her mind was made up before his last sentences put her face in flames.

"You are wrong," she could only murmur; "oh, you are dreadfully wrong!"

"I am right," he answered bitterly, "and *you* are right. No wonder you dread the hard things that would be said of you! Take away the name and the money, and what am I? A back-block larrikin — a common stockman!"

"The man for me," said Olivia hoarsely.

"Ah, yes, if I were not such a public match!"

"Whatever you are — whatever you may be — if you want me still ——"

"Want you! I have wanted you from the first. I shall want you till the last!"

Her reply was indistinct; her tears were falling fast; he took her two white hands, but even them he did not touch with his lips. A great silence held them both, and all the world; the island willows kissed the stream; in the sheet of gold beyond, a fish leapt, and the ripple reached the boat in one long thin fold. The girl spoke first.

"We need not be in a hurry to tell everybody," she began; but the words were retracted in the same breath. "What am I saying? Of course we will tell. Oh, what a contempt you must have for me!"

"I love you," he answered simply. "I am too happy to live. It's all too good to be true. Me of all men — the old bushman!"

She looked lovingly on his bearded and sunburnt face, shining as she had never seen it shine before.

"No; it's the other way about," she said. "I am not half good enough for you — you who were so brave yesterday in your trouble — who have been so simple always in your prosperity. It was enough to turn any one's head, but you — ah, I don't only love you. I admire you, dear; may God help me to make you happy!"

They stayed much longer on the lake, finally disembarking on its uttermost shore, because Olivia was curious to see how the hut would look in the first rosy light of her incredible happiness. And when they came to it, the sunlight glinted on the new iron roofing; the pine-trees exhaled their resin in the noon-day heat following the midnight rain; and the shadows were shot with golden shafts, where all was golden to the lovers' eyes.

Jack made a diffident swain; it was the girl who slipped her hand into his.

"You will never pull it down?" she said. "We will use it for a summer-house, and to remind you of your old life. And one day you will take me out to the Riverina, and show me the hut you really lived in, and all your old haunts. Oh, I shouldn't mind if we had both to go out there for good! A hut would take far less looking after than the Towers, and I should have you much more to myself. What fun it would be!"

Jack thought this a pretty speech, but the girl herself was made presently aware of its insincerity. They had retraced their steps, and there in front of them, cool and grey in the mellow August sunshine, with every buttress thrown up by its shadow, and the very spires perfectly reflected in the sleeping lake, stood the stately home which would be theirs for ever. Olivia saw it with a decidedly new thrill. She was looking on her future home, and yet her husband would be this simple fellow! Wealth could not cloy, nor grandeur overpower, with such a mate; that was perhaps the substance of her thought. It simplified itself next moment. What had she done to deserve such happiness? What could she ever do? And a possible tabernacle in the bush entered into neither question, nor engaged her fancy any more.

CHAPTER XVII

AN ANTI-TOXINE

THEY rowed over, and were in mid-water when the landau drove up to the house. It had been sent in for Mr. Dalrymple early in the forenoon. They saw nothing, however, until they landed, when the equipage was proceeding on its way to the stables, having deposited the guest. At this discovery, the Duke's excitement knew no bounds, so Olivia urged him to run on and leave her; and he took her advice, chiefly regretting that he had missed the proud moment of welcoming his old boss in the hall.

Jack regretted this the more when he reached the house. There was Dalrymple of Carara beginning his visit by roundly abusing the butler in the very portico! The guest was in a towering passion, the butler in a palsy of senile agitation; and between them on the step lay Dalrymple's Gladstone bag.

" What *is* the matter?" cried Jack, rushing

up with a very blank face. "Stebbings, what's this? What has he done, Mr. Dalrymple?"

"Refused to take in my bag! Says it's the footman's place!"

"Then what's he here for? The man must be drunk. Are you, Stebbings?"

The butler murmured an inarticulate reply.

"Get to your pantry, sir!" roared Jack. "You shall hear more of this when you are sober. Old servant or new servant, out you clear!"

And he took up the bag himself, as Stebbings gave a glassy stare and staggered off without a word.

"I'm extremely sorry for losing my temper," said Dalrymple, taking Jack's arm as they entered the house; "but it always was rather short, as I fear I needn't remind *you*. Really, though, your disgraceful old retainer would have provoked a saint. Drunk as fool in the middle of the day; drunk and insolent. Has the man been with you long?"

"Only fifty years or so with the family," replied Jack savagely; "but, by the living Lord, he may roll up his swag!"

"Ah! I wouldn't be hasty," said Dalrymple. "One must make allowances for one's old retainers; they're a privileged class. How good of you, by the way, to send in for me in such style! It prepared me for much. But I am bound to say it didn't prepare me for all this. No, I never should have pictured you in such an absolute palace had I not seen it with my own eyes!"

And now the visitor was so plainly impressed by all he saw, that Jack readily forgave him the liberty he had taken in rating Stebbings on his own account. Still the incident rankled. Dalrymple was the one man in the world before whom the Duke of St. Osmund's really did desire to play his new part creditably; and what could be said for a peer of the realm who kept a drunken butler to insult his guests? Jack could have shaken the old reprobate until the bones rattled again in his shrivelled skin. Dalrymple, however, seemed to think no more about the matter. He was entirely taken up with the suits of armour here in the hall: indeed Olivia discovered him lecturing Jack on his own trophies in a manner that would have led a stranger to mistake the guest for the host.

It may be said at once that this was Dalrymple's manner from first to last. It was that of the school-master to whom the boy who once trembled at his frown is a boy for evermore.

And it greatly irritated Jack's friends, though Jack himself saw nothing to resent.

The Duke led his guest into the great drawing-room, and introduced him with gusto to Lady Caroline Sellwood and to Claude Lafont. But all his pride was in the visitor, who, with his handsome cynical face, his distinguished bearing, and his faultless summer suit, should show them that at least one "perfect gentleman" could come out of Riverina. Jack waited a moment to enjoy the easy speeches and the quiet assurance of Dalrymple; then he left the squatter to Lady Caroline and to Claude. It was within a few minutes of the luncheon hour. Jack wanted a word with Stebbings alone. The more he thought of it, the less able was he to understand the old butler's extraordinary outbreak. Could he have been ill instead of drunk? A charitable explanation was just conceivable to Jack until he opened the pantry door; it fell to the ground that moment; for not only did he catch Stebbings in the act of filling a wine-glass with brandy, but the butler's breath was foul already with the spirit.

"Very well, my man," said Jack slowly. "Drink as much as you like! You'll hear from me when you're sober. But show so much as the tip of your nose in the dining-room, and I'll throw you through the window with my own hands!"

The upshot of the matter was indirect and a little startling; for this was the reason why Dalrymple of Carara took the head of his old hand's table at luncheon on the day of his arrival; and obviously it was Dalrymple's temporary occupation of that position, added to his unforgettable past relations with his host, which led him to behave exactly as though the table were his own.

A difficulty about the carving was the more immediate cause of the transposition. In the ordinary course, this was Stebbings's business, which he conducted on the sideboard with due skill; in his absence, however, the footmen had placed the dishes on the table; and as these included a brace of cold grouse, and neither Jack nor Claude was an even moderate practitioner with the carving-knife, there was a little hitch. Mr. Sellwood was not present; he took his lunch on the links; and Jack made no secret of his relief when the squatter offered to fill the breach.

"Capital!" he cried; "you take my place, sir, and I wish you joy of the billet." And so the thing fell out.

It had the merit of seating the Duke and Olivia side by side; and the happy pair were made distinctly happier by the mutual discovery that neither had as yet confided in a third soul. At the foot of the table, in the position which Jack had begged her to assume at the outset of her visit, sat Lady Caroline Sellwood. The clever young men were on opposite sides, as usual; nor did they fail to exchange those looks of neglected merit and of intellectual boredom which were another feature of their public appearances. Their visit had not been altogether a success. It was a mystery why they prolonged it. They had been invited, however, to spend a month at Maske Towers, which, after all, was neither an uncomfortable resting-place nor a discreditable temporary address.

Francis Freke said a Latin grace inaudibly, and then the squatter went to work at the birds. These were a present from afar; there were no moors "on" Maske, as Jack explained, with a proud eye on Dalrymple's knife. It flashed through the joints as though the bird had been already "boned"; on either side the breast fell away in creamy flakes; and Dalrymple talked as he carved, with the light touch and the easy grace of a many-sided man of the world. At first he seemed to join in everybody's conversation in turns; but he was only getting his team together; and in a little everybody was listening to him. Yet he talked with such tact that it was possible for all to put in their word; indeed, he would appeal first to one, then to another, so that the general temper of the party rose to a high level. Only Olivia and Claude Lafont felt that this stranger was taking rather much upon himself. Otherwise it was a pleasure to listen to him; he was excellently well informed; before the end of the meal it came out that he had actually read Claude's poems.

"And lived to tell the tale!" he added with characteristic familiarity. "I can tell you I felt it a risk after reading that terrible depreciation of you in the *Parthenon;* you see, I've been in England a few days, and have been getting abreast of things at my hotel while my tailors were making me externally presentable. By the way, I ran across a young Australian journalist who is over here now, and who occasionally scribbles for the *Parthenon.* I asked him if he knew who had made that scurrilous attack upon you, Mr. Lafont. I was interested, because I knew you must be one of Jack's relations."

"And did you find out?" inquired Claude, with pardonable curiosity.

"He found out for me. The culprit was a man of your name, Mr. Stubbs; no relation, I hope?"

"I hope not," said Stubbs, emptying his glass; and his pallid complexion turned a sicklier yellow, as though his blood were nicotine, and the nicotine had mounted to his face.

"I should like to hear that name in full," said Lady Caroline down the length of the table. "I read the article myself. It was a disgrace to journalism. It is only fair to our Mr. Stubbs that we should hear his namesake's Christian name."

"I think I can oblige," said Dalrymple, producing his pocket-book. "His name was — ah! here it is! His name was Edmund. Edmund Stubbs!"

Edmund Stubbs was not unequal to the occasion. He looked straight at Jack.

"Will you kindly make it convenient to send me in to Devenholme in time for the next train?" he said. "If the Australian — gentleman — is going to stay in your house, I, for one, shall trespass no longer on your hospitality."

"Nor I, for another!" Llewellyn chimed in.

And without further ceremony the mordant couple left the table and the room. Jack looked embarrassed, and Claude felt sorry for

Jack. As for Olivia, she had felt vaguely indignant with Dalrymple ever since he had taken the head of the table; and this scene put a point to her feelings, while it also revived her first prejudice against the squatter. Lady Caroline, however, congratulated him upon an excellent piece of work.

"You have performed a public service, my dear Mr. Dalrymple," said she. "Dear Jack will, I know, forgive me when I say that those two young men have never been in their element here. They are all right in a London drawing-room, as representatives of a certain type. In a country house they are impossible; and, for my part, I shall certainly never send them another card."

Jack also was ceasing to disapprove of the humiliation of Edmund Stubbs, whose remarks overnight in the Poet's Corner had suddenly recurred to his mind.

"Did you know it was the same man?" said he, pushing back his chair.

"I'm afraid I did," replied the squatter, as he rose. "They told me he was staying down here, and I could hardly avoid exposing the fellow. I hope, my dear Jack, that you will forgive the liberty I undoubtedly took in doing so. I am the germ that expels the other germs

—a sort of anti-toxine in cuffs. *Similia simili-bus*, if my memory serves me, Mr. Lafont. Before long you may have to inject a fresh bacillus to expel *me!* Meantime, my dear Jack, let me offer you a cigar to show there's no ill-feeling."

"No, thanks," said Jack, for once rather shortly; "you've got to smoke one of mine. It's my house!" he added, with a grin.

And the remark was much appreciated by those to whom it was not addressed; on Dalrymple it produced no effect at all.

CHAPTER XVIII

HECKLING A MINISTER

THE engagement became known in the course of the afternoon, and the news was received in a manner after all very gratifying to the happy pair. Lady Caroline Sellwood did indeed insist on kissing her future son-in-law, but the obvious attitude she now assumed did not impose upon him for a moment. He had seen through her the night before; he could never believe in the woman again. In any case, however, her affectation of blank surprise, and her motherly qualms concerning the prospective loss of her ewe lamb, were a little over-acted, even for so inexperienced an observer as the Duke of St. Osmund's. She knew it, too, and hated Jack with all her hollow heart for having found her out; to him, it was, after this, a relief to listen to the somewhat guarded observations of Mr. Sellwood, whose feelings in the matter were just a little mixed.

Of the rest, Francis Freke volunteered his

services for the great event, and both he and his wife (who brought down her entire speaking family to say good-night to " Uncle Jack ") were consumed with that genuine delight in the happiness of others which was their strongest point. Claude, too, was not only " very nice about it," as Olivia said, but his behaviour, in what was for him a rather delicate situation, showed both tact and self-control. Never for a moment did look or word of his suggest the unsuccessful suitor: though to be sure he had scarcely qualified for such a *rôle*. Olivia and he had never been more than friends. On her side, at least, the friendship had been of that perfectly frank and chronic character which is least likely to develop into love. And no one knew this better than Claude himself, who, moreover, was not even yet absolutely sure that his own undoubted affections were inspired by the divine impulse for which his poet's heart had so often yearned. At all events he had thought upon the one maiden for very many months; and putting it no higher than this, his present conduct was that of a tolerably magnanimous man.

The one person who raised an unsympathetic eyebrow was Dalrymple the squatter. He seemed surprised at the news and, for the moment, rather annoyed; but Jack recalled the deplorably cynical view of women for which the owner of Carara had been quite notorious in the back-blocks, and the squatter's displeasure did not rankle. Nor was it expressed a second time. Either the sight of the pair together, who made no secret of their happiness; either this pretty spectacle, or the dictates of good taste, moved Dalrymple, ultimately, to the most graceful congratulations they had yet received. And it was characteristic of the man that his remarks took the form of an unsolicited speech at the dinner-table.

He had been only a few hours in the house, yet to all but Mr. Sellwood (who did not meet him until evening) the hours seemed days. For the squatter was one of those men who carry with them the weight of their own presence, the breath of an intrinsic power, subtly felt from the first; thus the little house-party had taken more notice of him in one afternoon than the normal stranger would have attracted in a week; and to them it already seemed inevitable that he should lead and that they should follow whether they would or no. Accordingly, they were not in the least surprised to see Dalrymple on his legs when the crumb-cloth had been removed; though all but Jack deemed the act a liberty; and the squatter still adopted the tone of a master felicitating his men, rather than that of a guest congratulating his host.

Yet the speech was fluent and full of point; and the speaker himself made a sufficiently taking figure, leaning slightly forward, with the tips of his well-shaped fingers just resting on the black oak board that dimly reflected them. An unexceptionable shirt-front sat perfectly on his full, deep chest, a single pearl glistening in its centre; and there was a gleam of even teeth between the close-cropped, white moustache and the ugly, mobile, nether lip, whence every word fell distinct and clear of its predecessor. The Home Secretary had heard a worse delivery from his own front bench; and he was certainly interested in the story of the iron hut and the savages of Northern Queensland, which Dalrymple repeated with the happiest effect. Olivia forgave him certain earlier passages on the strength of these; her heart was full; only she could not lift her eyes from the simple chain about her wrist, for they were dim. The speech closed with the dramatic climax of the tale; there had been but one interruption to the flow of well-chosen words, and that was when the speaker stopped to blow out a smoking candle without appealing to his host.

The health of the pair was then drunk with appropriate enthusiasm; poor Jack blurted out a few honest words, hardly intelligible from his emotion; and the three ladies left the room.

"There's one more point to that yarn," said Dalrymple, closing the door he had held open, "that I don't think you yourself are aware of, Jack. It was when you got back to the store, with your shirt burnt off your back, and the country in a blaze all round, that I first noticed the legend on your chest. As you probably know, Mr. Sellwood, the Duke has one of his own eagles tattooed upon his chest. I saw it that day for the first time. I felt sure it meant something. And years afterwards, when I heard that a London solicitor was scouring the Colonies for the unknown Duke of St. Osmund's, it was the sudden recollection of that mark which made me to some extent the happy instrument of his discovery."

"To every extent!" cried Jack, wringing his benefactor's hand. "I've always said so. Mr. Sellwood, I owe him everything, and yet he makes a song about my scaring away a few blackfellows with a bush-fire! By the hokey, I've a good mind to have him live happily with us ever after for his pains!"

The Home Secretary bent his snowy head: his rosy face was the seat of that peculiarly grim expression with which political caricaturists have familiarised the world. Dalrymple's light eyes twinkled like polished flints; here was high game worthy of his gun. He took the empty chair on Mr. Sellwood's left.

"I understand, sir, that you are fatally bitten with golf?" began the squatter in his airiest manner. The other lit a cigarette with insolent deliberation before replying.

"I'm fond of the game," he said at length, "if that's what you mean."

"That was precisely what I did mean. Pardon me if I used an unparliamentary expression. I have read a great deal in your English papers —with which I never permit myself to lose touch —of the far-reaching ravages of the game. Certainly the disease must be widespread when one finds a Cabinet Minister down with the —golf!"

"We don't pronounce the *l*," Mr. Sellwood observed. "We call it *goff*." For though in political life an imperturbable temper was one of his most salient virtues, the Home Secretary was notoriously touchy on the subject of his only game.

Dalrymple laughed outright.

" A sure symptom, my dear sir, of a thoroughly dangerous case! But pray excuse my levity; I fear we become a little too addicted to chaff in the uncivilised wilds. I am honestly most curious about the game. I'm an old fogey myself, and I might like to take it up if it really has any merits —— "

"It has many," put in Claude cheerily, to divert an attack which Mr. Sellwood was quite certain to resent.

"Has it?" said the squatter incredulously. "For the life of one I can't see where those merits come in. To lay yourself out to hit a sitting ball! I'd as soon shoot a roosting hen!"

"Hear, hear!" cried Jack. "That's exactly what *I* say, Mr. Dalrymple."

The discussion had in fact assumed the constituent elements of a "foursome," which may have been the reason why the Home Secretary was unable any longer to maintain the silence of dignified disdain.

"I should like to take you out, the two of you," he said, "with a driver and a ball between you. I should like to see which of you would hit that sitting ball first, and how far!"

"We'll take you on to-morrow!" exclaimed Jack.

But the Home Secretary made no reply.

"I'm not keen," remarked Dalrymple. "It can't be a first-class game."

"You're hardly qualified to judge," snapped Sellwood, "since you've never played."

"Exactly why I *am* qualified. I'm not down with the disease."

"Then pray let us adopt the Duke's suggestion, and play a foursome to-morrow — like as we sit. Eh, Mr. — I beg your pardon, but I quite forget your name?"

"Dalrymple," replied the squatter; "and yours, once more?"

"Look in Whitaker," growled the Home Secretary, rising; and he left the table doubly angered by the weakness of his retort, where indeed it was weak to have replied at all.

Decidedly the squatter was no comfortable guest. Apart from his monstrous freedom of speech and action, which might pass perhaps on a bush station, but certainly not in an English country house, he was continually falling foul of somebody. Now it was the butler, now a fellow guest, and lastly a connection of his host, and one of Her Majesty's Ministers into the bargain. In each case, to be sure, the other side was primarily in the wrong. The butler was the worse for drink; the *Parthenon* man had indulged in gratuitous abuse of his friend; even Mr. Sellwood had taken amiss what was meant as pure chaff, and had been the first to begin the game of downright rudeness at which the old Australian had soon beaten him. Yet the fact remained that Dalrymple was the moving spirit in each unpleasantness; he had been a moving spirit since the moment he set foot in the house, and this was exactly what the other guests resented. But it was becoming painfully apparent that Jack himself would take nothing amiss; that he was constitutionally unable to regard Dalrymple in any other light than that of his old king, who could still do no wrong. And this being so, it was impossible for another to complain.

Indeed, when Mr. Sellwood joined the ladies, who happened to be in the conservatory, with savage words upon his lips, his wife stuck up for the maligned Colonist. That, however, was partly from the instinct of conjugal opposition, and partly because Lady Caroline was herself afraid of " this fellow Dalrymple," as her husband could call him fluently enough behind his back. The other men were not long in joining the indignant Minister. They had finished their cigarettes, but Jack had donned his gorgeous smoking-cap by special request

R

of Lady Caroline, who beamed upon him and it from her chair.

"Hallo! have you come in for that thing?" exclaimed Mr. Sellwood, who was in the mood to hail with delight any target for hostile criticism. "I always thought you intended it for Claude, my dear Caroline?"

"It turned out to be a little too small for Claude," replied her Ladyship sweetly.

"Claude, you've had an escape," said the Home Secretary. "Jack, my boy, you have my sympathy."

"I don't require it, thank you, sir," laughed the Duke. "I'm proud of myself, I tell you! This'd knock 'em up at Jumping Sandhills, wouldn't it, Mr. Dalrymple?"

"It would indeed: so the cap goes with the coronet, does it?" added the squatter, but with such good-humour that it was impossible to take open umbrage at his words. "I wonder how it would fit me?" And he lifted the thing off Jack's head by the golden tassel, and dropped it upon his own.

"Too small again," said Jack: indeed the purple monstrosity sat upon the massive hairless head like a thimble on a billiard-ball.

"And it doesn't suit you a bit," added Olivia, who was once more in a simmer of indignation with her lover's exasperating friend.

"No more would the coronet," replied Dalrymple, replacing the smoking-cap on its owner's head. "By the way, Jack, where do you keep your coronet?"

"Where do I keep my coronet?" asked the Duke of his major-domo. "I've never set eyes on it."

"I fancy they have it at the bank," said Claude.

"And much good it does you there!" exclaimed Dalrymple. "Shall I tell you what I'd do with it if it were mine?"

"Yes, do," said Jack, smiling in advance.

"Then come outside and you shall hear. I am afraid I have shocked your friends sufficiently for one night. And there's a very fascinating moon."

CHAPTER XIX

THE CAT AND THE MOUSE

"You're a lucky fellow," said the squatter as they sauntered down the drive. "Give me another of those cigars; they are better than mine, after all."

"They ought to be," replied Jack complacently. "I told old Claude to pay all he could for 'em."

"He seems to have done so. What an income you must have!"

"About fifteen bob a minute, so they tell me."

"After a pound a week in the bush!"

"It does sound rummy, doesn't it? After you with the match, sir."

"It's incredible."

"Yet it's astonishing how used you get to it in time — you'd be surprised! At first the whole thing knocked me sideways; it was tucker I couldn't digest. But once you take to the soft tack, there's nothing like it in the world. You may guess who's made me take to it quicker than I might have done!"

Dalrymple shrugged his massive shoulders, and raised a contemplative eye to the moon, that lay curled like a silver shaving in the lucid heavens.

"Oh, yes, I can guess," he said sardonically. "And mind you I've nothing against the girl — I meant you were lucky there. The girl's all right — if you must marry. I don't dislike a woman who'll show fight; and she looked like showing it when I tried on that cracker-night-cap thing of yours. Oh, certainly! If you were to marry, you couldn't have done better; the girl's worth fifty of her mother, at any rate."

"Fifty million!" cried Jack, somewhat warmly.

"Fifty million I meant to say," and the squatter ran his arm through that of his host. "Come, don't you mind *me*, Jack, my boy! You know what an old heathen I am in those little matters; and we have lots of other things to talk about, in any case."

Jack was mollified in a moment.

"Lots!" he cried. "I don't seem to have seen anything of you yet, and I'm sure you haven't seen much of the place. Isn't it a place and a half? Look at the terrace in the moonlight — and the spires — and the windows — hundreds of 'em — and the lawn and the tank!

Then there's the inside; you've seen the hall; but I must show you the picture-gallery and the State Apartments. Such pictures! They say it's one of the finest private collections in the world; there's hardly one of them that isn't by some old master or another. I've heard the pictures alone are worth half a million of money!"

"They are," said Dalrymple.

"You've heard so too?"

"Of course; my good fellow, your possessions are celebrated all the world over; that's what you don't appear to have realised yet."

"I can't," said Jack. "It puts me in a sick funk when I try! So it would you if you were suddenly to come in for a windfall like mine — that is, if you were a chap like me. But you aren't; you'd be the very man for the billet."

And Jack stepped back to admire his hero, who chuckled softly as he smoked, standing at his full height, with both hands in his pockets, and the moon like limelight on his shirt.

"It's not a billet I should care about," said the squatter; "but it's great fun to find you filling it so admirably ——"

"I don't; I wish I did," said Jack, throwing away the cigar which he had lighted to keep his guest company.

" You do, though. And if it isn't a rude question —— " Dalrymple hesitated, staring hard — " I daresay you're very happy in your new life? "

" Of course I'm very happy *now*. None happier! "

" But apart from the girl? "

" You can't get apart from her; that's just it. If I'm to go on being happy in my position, I'll have to learn to fill it without making myself a laughing-stock; and the one person who can teach me will be my wife. "

" I see. Then you begin to like your position for its own sake? "

" That's so, " replied Jack. He was paring a cake of very black tobacco for the pipe which he had stuck between his teeth. Dalrymple watched him with interest.

" And yet, " said the squatter, " you have neither acquired a taste for your own most excellent cigars, nor conquered your addiction to the vile twist we used to keep on the station ! "

" Well, and that's so, too, " laughed Jack. " You must give a fellow time, Mr. Dalrymple ! "

" Do you know what I thought when I met you yesterday? " continued Dalrymple, turning his back to the moon, and looking very hard at Jack while he sucked at his cigar with his thick, strong lips. " Do you know how you struck me then? I thought you'd neither acquired a taste for your new life nor conquered your affection for the old. That's how you struck me in Devenholme yesterday."

Jack made no haste to reply. He was not at all astonished at the impression he had created the day before. But his old boss was still the one man before whom he was anxious to display a modicum of dignity, even at the expense of a pose. And it is noteworthy that he had neither confided in Dalrymple concerning his dilemma of the previous day, nor yet so much as mentioned in his hearing the model hut among the pines.

"I don't wonder," he said at length; "it was the way I was likely to strike you just then. Don't you see? I hadn't got it out at the time!"

"So it was only the girl that was on your nerves?" said Dalrymple in disgust.

"And wasn't that enough? If I'm a different man to-day, you know the reason why. As for being happy in my position, and all that, I'm simply in paradise at this moment. Think of it! Think of me as I was, and look at me as I am; think of my little hut on Carara, and look behind you at Maske Towers!"

They were on the terrace now, leaning idly

against the balustrade. Dalrymple turned and looked: like Melrose Abbey, the grand grey building was at its best in the "pale moonlight"; the lichened embrasures met the soft sky softly; the piercing spires were sheathed in darkness; and the mountainous pile wore one uniform tint, from which the lighted windows stood out like pictures on a wall. Dalrymple looked, and looked again; then his hard eyes fell upon the rude ecstasy of the face beside him; and they were less hard than before.

"You may make yourself easy," said the squatter. "I shan't stay long."

"What the blazes do you mean?" cried Jack. "I want you to stay as long as ever you can."

"You may; your friends do not."

"Hang my friends!"

"I should enjoy nothing better; but it isn't practicable. Besides, they're a good deal more than your friends now; they are — her people. And they don't like the man who was once your boss; he offends their pride ——"

"Mr. Dalrymple ——"

"Enough said, my boy. I know my room, and I'm going to turn in. We'll talk it over again in the morning; but my mind is made up. Good-night!"

"I'll come in with you."

“ As you like.”

They parted at the visitor’s door.

“ You’ll disappoint me cruel if you *do* go,” said Jack, shaking hands. “ I’m quite sure you’re mistaken about my friends; Olivia, for one, thinks no end of you. However, as you say, we can talk it over in the morning — when you’ve got to see the pictures as well, and don’t you forget it! So long, sir, till then.”

“ So long, Jack. I’ll be your man in the morning, at all events. And I shall look forward to a great treat in your famous picture-gallery.”

But Jack was engaged; and he realised it in the morning as he had not done before. Olivia lured him from the squatter’s side; she had every intention of so doing. The pair went for a little stroll. Neither wore a watch; the little stroll lengthened into miles; it carried them beyond the sound of the stable clock; they forgot the world, and were absurdly late for lunch. Lady Caroline Sellwood had taken it upon herself to conduct the meal without them. Dalrymple was in his place; his expression was grimly cynical; he had seen the pictures, under Claude Lafont’s skilled escort, and, with the ladies’ permission, he would now leave the table, as he had still to put in his things.

His things! Was he going, then? Jack's knife and fork fell with a clatter.

"I thought you knew," said Claude. "He is going up to town by the afternoon train. I have ordered the landau, as I thought you would like him to go as he came."

When Jack heard this he, too, left the table, and bounded upstairs. He found Dalrymple on the point of packing his dress-clothes, with the assistance of none other than Stebbings. Jack glared at the disrated butler, and ordered him out of the room.

"I wouldn't have done that," remarked the squatter, pausing in his work. "The fellow came to know if he could do anything for me, with tears in his eyes, and he has made me a handsome apology. He didn't ask me to beg him off, but I mean to try my luck in that way before I go."

"You mustn't go!"

"I must. Will you forgive the old man?"

"Not if you clear."

"My good fellow, this is unreasonable ——"

"So it is, Mr. Dalrymple, on *your* part," rejoined Jack warmly. "It's too bad of you. Bother Stebbings! I shan't be hard on him, you may be sure; and you mustn't be hard on me. Surely you can make allowances for a chap who's engaged to a girl like mine? I *did* want to speak to you this morning; but she came first. I want to speak to you now — more than you suppose. Mr. Dalrymple, I wasn't straight with you last night; not altogether. But I can't suffer steering crooked; it gives me the hump; and as sure as I do it I've got to go over the ground again. You are the man I owe my all to; I can't end up crooked with *you!*"

Dalrymple sat on the bedside in his shirt-sleeves; he had turned up the cuffs; his strong and shapely wrists lay along his thighs; and his grey eyebrows, but not his lips, asked for more.

"I mean," continued Jack, "about what was bothering me that day I ran against you in Devenholme. It was only the day before yesterday, but Lord! it seems like the week before last."

And with that he unfolded, with much rapid detail, the whole episode of Matthew Hunt, from the morning in the stable-yard to the midnight at the hut. The story within that story was also told with particular care and circumstance; but long before the end was reached Dalrymple had emptied his bag upon the bed, and had himself rung to countermand the carriage. He was interested; he would stay another day.

Downstairs in the drawing-room the Sellwood family and Claude Lafont were even then congratulating themselves upon the imminent departure of the unpopular guest. Their faces were so many sights when Jack entered in the highest spirits to tell them of his successful appeal to the better feelings of "good old Dalrymple," who after all was not going to leave them just yet. Jack was out again in an instant; and they next saw him, from the drawing-room windows, going in the direction of the hut with his odious old friend at his side. Whereupon Claude Lafont said a strong thing, for him; and the most sensible of engaged young women retired in tears to her room.

"There's one thing you must let me do," Dalrymple was saying; "if you don't, I shall insist. You must let me have the privilege of sorting that scoundrel, Mark Hunt."

"Matthew," said Jack.

"Matthew, then. I knew it was one of you evangelists."

"What would you do?" asked the Duke.

"See that he annoyed you no more. And I'll guarantee that he doesn't if you'll leave him to me."

"I didn't want to clear them out ——"

"I think you must."

"Or to prosecute; it's so public, and a bit revengeful too."

"There I agree with you. I'm not even sure that you'd get a conviction. It would be difficult, in any case, and would make a public scandal of it, as you say."

"Then I will leave him to you. You're the smartest man I know, Mr. Dalrymple, and always have been. What you do will be right. I'll bother my head no more about it. Besides, anything to keep you with us a few days longer!"

Dalrymple shrugged his shoulders, but Jack did not see the gesture, for he was leading the way through the pines. A moment later they were at the hut.

The hut amused the squatter. He called it a colourable imitation. But it did not delight him as it had delighted Jack; the master bushman failed to share his old hand's sentimental regard for all that pertained to the bush. Dalrymple sat on the bunk and smoked a cigar, a cynical spectator of some simple passages between Jack and his cats. Livingstone was exhibited with great pride; he had put on flesh in the old country; at which the squatter remarked that had he stayed on Carara, he would have put on an ounce of lead.

"You're a wonderful man, Jack!" he exclaimed at length. "I wouldn't have believed a fellow *could* take a windfall as you have done, if I hadn't seen it with my own eyes. I used to think of you a good deal after you had gone. I thought of you playing the deuce to any extent, but I must say I little dreamt of your building a bush hut to get back to your old way of life! I pictured the town crimson and the country carmine — both painted by you — but I never imagined *this!*"

And he looked round the hut in his amused, sardonic way; but there was a ring — or perhaps it was only a suspicion — of disappointment in his tone. The next words were merely perplexed.

"And yet," added Dalrymple, "you profess yourself well pleased with your lot!"

"So I am — now."

"I begin to wish I hadn't changed my mind about going this afternoon."

"Why, on earth?"

"Because I also begin — to envy you! Come, let's make tracks for the house; I shall have huts enough to look at when I go back to the place that you need never see again."

"But I mean to see it again," said Jack as he locked up. "I intend to take my wife out, one

of these days; we shall expect to come on a
long visit to Carara; and the greatest treat you
could give me would be to let me ride my old
boundaries and camp in my old hut for a week!"

"Nonsense; you stay where you are," was
the squatter's only comment. He seemed depressed; his cynical aplomb had quite deserted
him. They returned in silence to the house.

A shabby-looking vehicle stood in front of
the porch; the man said that he had brought
a gentleman from Devenholme, and was to wait.
The Duke and Dalrymple mounted the steps
together. The first person they encountered in
the hall was Claude Lafont, looking strangely
scared; but a new-comer was in the act of taking off his coat; and, as he turned his face,
Dalrymple and Jack started simultaneously.
Both knew the man. It was Cripps the lawyer. And he, too, looked pale, nervous, and
alarmed.

CHAPTER XX

"LOVE THE DEBT"

OLIVIA was not a little tired; this was the true explanation of the tears which had driven her upstairs. It was also the one excuse she saw for herself when she thought the matter over in her own room. Jack had devoted the whole morning to her; it was the squatter's turn; and, of course, Jack must invite whom he liked to stay as long as he pleased. To think of limiting his freedom in any such matter at the very outset of their engagement! Yet she had been guilty of that thought; but she was tired; she would lie down for an hour.

She lay down for two or three. Excitement had worn her out. It was after five when she awoke and went downstairs. As she did so Claude and Cripps crossed the hall and put on their hats. She hailed Claude.

"What have you done with Jack?"

"I think you'll find him in the little study at the end of the library."

"Thanks."

Olivia glanced at Cripps. She had never met him. She wondered who he was, and why Claude did not introduce him to her, and what made both of them so glum. They hurried out of the house as though they were afraid of her. What could it mean? She would find out from Jack; she felt a renewed right to him now, and thought of hints, as she went, for Mr. Dalrymple, if they were still together. But Jack was alone; he was sitting in the dejected attitude engendered by a peculiarly long and low arm-chair.

"Well?" said Olivia briskly.

"Well?" responded Jack; but he looked at her without rising and without a smile; and both omissions were unlike the lover and the man.

"I half expected to find Mr. Dalrymple with you. I'm so glad he isn't! I—it's my turn, I think!"

"I haven't seen Dalrymple for over an hour," said Jack, with his heavy, absent eyes upon her all the time. "I wonder where he is?"

Olivia would not ask him what the matter was; she preferred to find out for herself, and then tell *him*. She looked about her. On a salver were a decanter and three wine-glasses; one was unused; and on the floor there lay an end of pink tape. She picked and held it up between finger and thumb.

"Lawyers!" she cried.

"Yes, I've had a solicitor here."

"Not to make your will!"

"No. On a—on a local matter. Don't look at me like that! It's nothing much: nothing new, at all events."

"But you are worried."

She knelt beside his chair, and rested her elbows on the arm, studying his pale set profile. His eyes met hers no longer.

"I am," he admitted: "but that's my own fault. As I say — it's nothing new!"

"Who was the lawyer?"

"You wouldn't know him."

"I mean to know who he was. Mr. Cripps?"

Jack did not answer. He rolled his head from side to side against the back of the chair. His eyes remained fast upon the opposite wall.

"It is — the old trouble," Olivia whispered. "The trouble of two nights ago!"

His silence told her much. The drops upon his forehead added more. Yet her voice was calm and undismayed; it enabled him at last to use his own.

"Yes!" he said hoarsely. "Claude made a mistake. It was true after all!"

"Hunt's story, darling?"

"Hunt's story. There *was* an English marriage as well as an Australian one. He had a wife at each side of the world! Claude made a mistake. He went to the wrong church at Chelsea — to a church by the river. He had always thought it was the parish church. It is not. St. Luke's is the parish church, and there in the book they have the marriage down in black and white. Cripps found it; but he first found it somewhere else, where he says they have the records of every marriage in the country since 1850. He would have looked there the day Claude was up, but he left it too late. He looked yesterday, and found it, sure enough, on the date Hunt gave. October 22d, 1853. And he has been to Chelsea and seen it there. So there's no mistake about it this time; and you see how we stand."

"I see. My poor boy!"

"It's Claude after all. Poor chap, he's awfully cut up. He blames himself so for the mistake between the two churches; but Cripps tells me it was the most natural mistake in the world. Chelsea Old Church — that was where Claude went. And he says he'll never forgive himself."

"But I forgive him," said Olivia, with the first sign of emotion in her voice. She was holding one of his hands; her other was in his hair. Still he stared straight in front of him.

" Of course you forgive him," he said gently. " When you come to think of it, there's nothing to forgive. Claude didn't make the facts. He only failed to discover them."

" I am glad he *did* fail," whispered Olivia.

" Glad? You can't be glad! Why do you say that?"

And now he turned his face to her, in his astonishment; and suddenly it was she who could not meet his gaze.

" How can you be glad?" he continued to demand.

" Because — otherwise — you would never — have — spoken —— "

" Spoken? Of course I shouldn't! It's a thousand pities I did. It makes it all the harder —now!"

" What do you mean?"

" Surely you see?"

They had risen with a common instinct. The ice was broken; there were no more shamefaced glances. The girl stood proudly at her full height.

" I see nothing. You say our engagement makes this all the harder for you; it *should* be just the opposite."

"Will nothing make you see?" cried Jack. "Oh, how am I to say it? It — it can't go on — our engagement!"

"And why not?"

"I am nothing — nobody — a nameless ——"

"What does it matter?" interrupted Olivia passionately. "Do you really think it was the name I wanted after all? You pay me a high compliment! I know exactly what you mean — know exactly what this means to you. To me it makes no difference at all. You are the man you have always been; you are the man — I — love."

His eyes glistened.

"God bless you for saying so! You are the one to love a man the better when he's down on his luck. I know that. Yet we must never ——"

"Never what?"

"Marry."

"Not — marry?" She stared at him in sheer amazement. "Not when we promised — only yesterday? You may break your word if you like. Mine I would never break!"

"Then I must. It is not to be thought of any more. Surely you see? It's not that I have lost the money and the title; oh! you must see what it is!"

"Of course I see. But I don't allow the objection."

"Your people would never hear of it now; and quite right too."

"My people! I am of age. I have a little money of my own, enough for us both. I can do exactly what I like. Besides, I'm not so sure about my people; you don't know my father as I know him."

"He is a man of the world. He would not hear of it."

"Then I must act for myself."

"You must not!"

"I must. Do you think I am only a fair-weather girl? I gave you my promise when all was different. I would rather die than break it now."

"But I release you! I set you free! Everything has altered. Oh, can't you put yourself in my place? I should deserve shooting if I married you now. I release you because I must."

"And I refuse to be released."

They regarded one another with hopeless faces. Their eyes were dim with love — yet here they stood apart. This was the dead-lock. Nothing could come of this contest of honour against honour, of one unselfish love against another. It was like striking flint upon flint, and steel upon steel. A gong sounded in the distance; it was the signal to dress for dinner. Olivia beat the floor impatiently with one foot; her lips trembled; her eyes filled with tears.

"If you cared for me," she cried passionately, "half as much as you said you did, you wouldn't be so ready to lose me now!"

"If I cared less," he answered, "I would take you at your word — God knows how you tempt me to! — and you should be my wife in spite of all. I would mind less how I dragged you down — what became of us in the end. But I love you too well to spoil your life. Don't you know that, Olivia?"

"Ah, yes! I know it! I know — I know ——"

He took her in his arms at last. He was shaking all over. Her head lay back upon his shoulder. He smoothed the hair from the high, white forehead; he looked tenderly and long into the wild wet eyes. His arm tightened about her; he could not help it.

"Sweetheart," he faltered, "you must help me to be strong. It is hard enough as it is. Only help me, or it will be far harder. Help me now — at dinner. I am going to take the head of the table for the last time. Help me by being bright! We can talk afterwards. There is time enough. Only help me now!"

"I will do my best," whispered Olivia, disengaging herself from his trembling arms. "I will try to be as brave as you. Oh, there is no one in the world like you! Yes, do let us talk about it afterwards; there is so much to say and to decide. But I give you fair warning: I shall never — never — never let you go. Darling, you will need me now! And I cannot give you up — much less after this. Shall I tell you why? You have gone the wrong way to work; you have made me love you more than ever — my hero — my darling — my all!"

She stood a moment at the open door, kissing her hand to him — a rosy flush upon her face — the great tears standing in her eyes. Then she was gone. He watched her down the length of the library; the stained windows dappled her, as she passed, with rubies and sapphires, huge and watery; at the farther door she turned, and kissed her hand again — and fled.

CHAPTER XXI

THE BAR SINISTER

IT was a close night; the men were smoking their cigarettes on the terrace. Cripps was one of them; he was staying the night; he wished himself a hundred miles away. But Francis Freke took him in hand; they disappeared together, and a minute later the billiard-room windows burnt out of the night.

Mr. Sellwood was left a little in the cold. Claude and Jack were pacing the terrace with linked arms and lowered voices, and he wished to speak to Jack. Mr. Sellwood knew all. He was deeply sorry for Jack, for whom he had done his best at dinner by talking incessantly from grace to grace. The Home Secretary could be immensely entertaining when he chose. He had chosen to-night, as much for his daughter's sake as for Jack's. Olivia was his favourite child.

But then Dalrymple had not been there to heckle and insult his superior; he was gone nobody knew where. Not that he was gone for good, the luck stopped short of that. It appeared, however, that he had been excluded by a majority of two to one from the triangular council in the Poet's Corner. Since then he had not been seen; but his bag was still in his room, and it was only another of his liberties to absent himself from dinner without a word.

Olivia was playing the piano in the drawing-room. The windows were wide open, and Mr. Sellwood listened with his white head bent in sorrowful perplexity. The execution was faulty, as usual, because Olivia was an idle musician; but there was feeling in her fingers, she had a certain "touch," and her attempts were better to listen to than some performances. To-night they went to her father's heart. The imperfect music spoke to him with the eloquence of broken words. It told him of his child's necessity for action in the stress of her anguish. It told him also of her love; and here was this poor fellow so taken up with Claude that it was impossible to say to him what must be said as soon as possible.

Mr. Sellwood gave it up for the present, and went to look for his wife.

"There's only one more thing, old man," Jack was saying, "and then I'm done. I don't want to load you up to the eyes with messages and all that. But I should like you to take care of this little bit of a key, and give it to her as soon as ever you think fit. It belongs to that chain bracelet business I got her for her birthday. As you know, I first wanted to give her a ring, but she wouldn't have it; and when I changed it for the bracelet, which cost about half as many shillings as the ring did pounds, I couldn't look poor Hopgood in the face. It was such a sell for him. So we were going back to-morrow to get that ring for our engagement, and to look old Hopgood in the face. That was one of our plans; we made so many when we were out this morning! I never knew a morning go at such a lick. But I remember it all — I remember everything. I've started going over every word we've said, so that I shan't forget anything. There's not such a vast lot to keep in your head. Only a day and a half of an engagement; but I've got to live on those thirty odd hours for the rest of my time."

Claude looked away; the drawing-room windows were a blur to his eyes; and Olivia's erratic rendering of Chopin filled in the pause. It was the incoherent expression of unutterable emotion. Jack listened also, nodding time with his head. The calmness and the nobility of despair had settled on his spirit, as on that of a captain going down with his ship.

He talked on, and his tone was entirely his own. It was neither bitter, querulous, nor wilfully pathetic; but chiefly contemplative, with a reminiscence here and the discovery of some consolation there. He recalled the humours of the situation, and laughed outright but staccato, as at remembered sayings of the newly dead. Beyond the loss of Olivia he had little to regret; even that would make another man of him for ever and a day. (So he talked.) And his English summer would be something to look back on always; it was pleasure to the good, which nothing could undo or take away; the experience of a second lifetime had been crammed into those few weeks. Let him remember that when he got back to the bush. Suppose he had never left the bush? Then he would never have seen the old country, and seen it (as he said) from the front seats; he would never have found his own soul, nor known the love of a lovely girl, nor the joy of life as he knew it now. So he was really to be congratulated to the end; there was no occasion to pity him at all.

Claude, however, was not comforted; he had

never been so wretched in his life. And he
showed it so plainly, and was withal so conscious of the display, that he felt quite sure
that Jack's ingenious consolations were not
meant entirely for Jack. He was ashamed of
himself on this, as on every other score. He
was to blame for the whole business, since it
was he who had scoured Australia for the Red
Marquis's son.   Nor could he believe the other's
protestations of personal solace and resignation;
they had been made with wistful glances at
the lighted windows, glances that Claude had
seen as they both leant back against the balustrade.

"Aha!" said Jack suddenly. "Here are Mr.
Sellwood and Lady Caroline coming to have
it out with me. Better leave me to them, old
man."

"All right," said Claude, "but we have lots
more to talk about. Where can I find you, and
when?"

Jack hesitated; the Sellwoods were within
earshot as he whispered, "Twelve o'clock at the
hut!" And Claude walked away, with his
hand aching from a sudden and most crushing
grip.

"My wife and I would like to speak to you,"
said the Home Secretary, halting in front of

Jack with Lady Caroline on his arm. "My dear fellow, we are so very sorry for you: we know everything."

"Everything!" echoed Lady Caroline, with slow dramatic force.

"Thanks to Jack," put in her husband sharply; "it was he who gave instructions that we should be told at once. It was so very good of you, Jack, my boy, to think of us in your trouble. You have behaved splendidly all through; that's what makes us all feel this so keenly; and I am quite sure that you will behave nobly now. My dear fellow, it isn't the fact of your not being the Duke of St. Osmund's that forces me to take this tone; it's the unfortunate circumstances of your birth, which have now been proved, I am afraid, beyond the possibility of that doubt which nobody would welcome more thankfully than myself. We are all very fond of you. I for one have learned to admire you too. But this most miserable discovery must alter everything except our feeling towards you. We are bound to consider our daughter."

"Our youngest child," said Lady Caroline. "Our ewe lamb!"

"Of course," replied Jack. "I see what you mean. What do you want me to do?"

"It may seem very hard," said Mr. Sellwood,

"but we wish you to release Olivia from her engagement."

"To release her instantly!" cried Lady Caroline.

"I have done that already," said Jack with some disdain. "Did you really think, sir, that I should wait to be told?"

Mr. Sellwood muttered an oath as he held out his hand.

"I have made a mistake; I hope you will forgive me," he said; and his hand was crushed in its turn.

"And what did she say?" asked Lady Caroline.

"She refused to be released."

"I knew it! George, the girl is mad. And pray what do you propose to do now?"

"What do you think I ought to do?"

"Ought?" cried Lady Caroline. "I think you ought to go away and never see her again!"

"Or, rather, let us take her away," said Mr. Sellwood. "It may seem hard and abominable, but there's no doubt that from our point of view a separation is the most desirable course."

"It *is* hard," replied Jack; "but, as it happens, it's the very plan I hit on for myself. Not a word, sir, if you please. You're perfectly right. She could not marry me now; and I would not marry her, knowing what I am. It's out of the question altogether. But Olivia is quite on to do it — at least she thought she was before dinner. I haven't seen her since. I'm not going to see her again. She's just the sort of angel who would swap heaven for hell to stand by the man she was fond of! But she mustn't be let. I agree with you there. It was the first thing I thought of myself. I made up my mind to clear out; and, if you want to know, I'm off now."

" Now ! " cried Mr. Sellwood.

Lady Caroline said nothing.

" Yes, now; there's no more to be said; and the sooner I get it over the better for all concerned."

" But, my dear fellow, where are you going, and what do you intend to do? Have you made any plans? I wouldn't do anything in a hurry if I were you; we're a family party here; and all our wits put together would surely be better than yours! We might fix up something between us."

Jack shook his head.

" You're very kind," he said; " but it's all fixed up. I'm going straight back to the bush. This is Thursday; I can't catch to-morrow's steamer, but I can do better. I can take the overland express to-morrow night, and join last week's boat at Brindisi. I'm going to sleep the night — never mind where. I don't want old Claude on my tracks; I've said good-bye to him too, though he doesn't know it either. He wants to do too much for me altogether. If you stay up with him till twelve, he'll tell you he's got to look me up at the hut; and you may tell him, sir, if you'll be so good, to sit tight, for he won't find me *there*. Say good-bye to him for me, and tell him he's been the best mate I've ever struck; but don't let him come up and see me off. Cripps I'm to meet in town. I'm going to let them finance me out again, since they fetched me home in the beginning; but not another red cent will I touch. Why should I? I've had a good run for my money — that is, for theirs. I'm no worse off than I was before. I should even be sure of the same old billet on Carara that used to suit me well enough, if I only could see Mr. Dalrymple before I start; but I'm bothered if I know where he's got to."

Mr. Sellwood was heavy with thought; his wife had left them; and he had heard a sob in her throat as she turned away. He had an inkling of her treatment of this poor fellow; he did not know everything, but he knew enough to hail his wife's sob with a thankful thrill. So there

was a heart in her somewhere still! He had
thought otherwise for some years; in another
moment he doubted it once more. Lady Caroline appeared at the drawing-room window, shut
it, and drew down the blind. And yet — and
yet her husband had himself been wishing for
somebody to do that very thing!

Olivia was still at the piano, and her perform-
ance had sounded a little too near at hand until
now. It was near enough still; but the shutting of the window deadened the sound. Chopin
had merged into Mendelssohn. Olivia happened
to be note-perfect in one or two of the Lieder.
Her father had never heard her play them so
well. But Jack had no music in his soul —
could not whistle two bars in tune — and though,
even while speaking, he listened visibly, it was
not to the music as music, but to the last sound
of Olivia he was ever to hear. Her footstep in
the distance would have done as well.

"I wouldn't go to-night, old fellow," the Home
Secretary said at length. "I see no point in it.
To-morrow would be time enough."

"Ah, you must think I find it easy work!"
exclaimed Jack, a little bitterly for once. "It's
not so easy as all that: it's got to be done
at once, when you're screwed up to it, or it may
never come off at all. Don't you try to keep

me; don't let anybody else try either! Let me go while I'm on to go — alone. I might take it different to-morrow!"

He spoke hoarsely; the voice was as significant as the words. Mr. Sellwood was impressed by both; he followed the other to the nearest flight of steps leading down to the lawn.

"Let me come with you," he urged. "Surely there is something one can do! And I've never seen the hut; I should like to."

"Wait till I've gone," was the reply. "I want you to stand in my tracks and block anybody from following me. Head them another way! Only give me quarter of an hour to clear out of the hut, and another quarter's start, and I'm — and I'm —— "

He lost himself in a sudden absence of mind. The music had stopped, and the night seemed insolently still. Jack was half-way down the steps; the Home Secretary leaned over the balustrade above. Jack reached up his hand.

"Good-bye," he said.

Mr. Sellwood, hesitating, kept his hand. The window that had been shut was thrown up again.

"Papa, is that you?"

"Yes, my dear."

Mr. Sellwood had turned round.

"And where is Jack?"

“Not here,” whispered Jack.

“Not here,” repeated Mr. Sellwood; and, looking behind him, he found that he had spoken the truth.

“Then I’m coming down to you, and you must help me —— ”

Jack lost the rest as he ran. He thought he heard his own name again, but he was not sure. He stopped under the nearest tree. Mercifully there was no moon. Olivia could not have seen him, for he himself could see no more of the Towers than the lighted windows and their reflections upon the terrace. On that dim stage the silhouette of Mr. Sellwood was still discernible: another joined it: the two figures became one: and in the utter stillness not only the girl’s sobs but her father’s broken words were audible under the tree.

Jack fled.

He ran hard to the hut, and lighted it up as it had never been lighted before. He cut up a candle in half-inch sections, and stuck them all over with their own grease. Thoroughness was an object as well as despatch; nothing must be missed; but his first act was to change his clothes. He put on the ready-made suit and the wideawake in which he had landed; he had kept them in the hut. Then he pulled from under the bunk the cage his cats had travelled in, and he bundled the cats into it once more. Lastly he rolled up his swag, less neatly, perhaps, than of old, but with the blue blanket outermost as before, and the little straps reefed round it and buckled tight. He would want these things in the bush ; besides, the whim was upon him to go exactly as he had come. Only one item of his original impedimenta he decided to leave behind : the old bush saddle would be a needless encumbrance ; but with his swag, and his cats, and his wideawake, he set forth duly, after blowing out all the candle ends.

The night seemed darker than ever ; neither moon nor star was to be seen, and Jack had to stop and consider when he got outside. He desired to strike a straight line to the gates ; he knew how they lay from the hut, though he had never been over the ground before. To a bushman, however, even without a star to help him, such a task could present no difficulties. He computed the distance at something less than a mile ; but in Australia he had gone as the crow flies through league upon league of untrodden scrub. Out there he had enjoyed the reputation of being "a good bushman," and he meant to enjoy it again.

But his head was hot with other thoughts, and he was out of practice. Instead of hitting the wall, and following it up to the gates, as he intended, he erred the other way, and came out upon the drive at no great distance from the house. This was a false start, indeed, and a humiliation also; but his thoughts had strayed back to Olivia, and it was as if his feet had followed their lead. He would think of her no more to-night.

The drive was undesirable, for obvious reasons; still it was the safest policy to keep to it now, and the chances were that he would meet nobody. Yet he did; a footstep first, and then the striking of a match, came to his ears as he was nearing the gates. He crept under the trees. The match was struck again, and yet again, before it lit. Then Jack came out of hiding, and strode forward without further qualms, for the flame was lighting the cigar and illumining the face of his friend Dalrymple.

"Hallo, sir!" began Jack, "I'd given you up."

"Why, Jack, is that you? I can't see an inch front of my cigar," said the squatter, as the match burnt itself out on the gravel where it had been thrown.

"Yes, it's me; where have you been?"

“Where are you going?”

“Mine first,” said Jack.

“All right. I’ve been talking to Master Hunt. *Now* where are you going?”

“Back to Australia!”

Jack waited for an exclamation; for some seconds there was none; then the squatter laughed softly to himself.

“I thought as much!” said he. “I knew exactly what the lawyer came to say, for I saw it in his face. Now tell me, and we’ll see if I’m right.”

And it appeared that he was, by the way in which he kept nodding his head as Jack told him all. Meanwhile they had retired under the trees, and by the red end of his cigar the squatter had seen Jack’s wideawake; using his cigar as a lantern he had examined the cage of cats; whereon his face would have proved a sufficiently severe commentary had there been any other light for Jack to see it by.

“Now,” said Dalrymple, “stand tight. *I’ve* got something to tell *you*, my boy!” And he told it in the fewest whispered words.

Jack was speechless.

“Nonsense! I don’t believe it,” he cried when he found his tongue.

“But I’m in a position to prove it,” replied

the squatter. " I'll give you a particular or two
as we walk back to the house. What! you
hesitate? Come, come; surely my word is good
enough for that! Do be sensible; leave your
infernal cats where they are, and come you along
with me!"

CHAPTER XXII

DE MORTUIS

THE Home Secretary had never spent a more
uncomfortable hour. His favourite daughter
had stanched her tears, and gone straight to the
root of the very delicate matter at issue between
them. Much as her tears had depressed him,
however, Mr. Sellwood preferred them to the
subsequent attitude. It was too independent
for his old-fashioned notions, and yet it made
him think all the more of Olivia. Indeed she
was her father's child in argument—spirited and
keen and fair. His point of view she took for
granted, and proceeded to expound her own.
Much that she said was unanswerable; a little
made him fidget—for between the sexes there
is no such shyness as that which a father finds
in his heart towards his grown-up girls. But a
certain bluntness of speech was not the least
refreshing trait in Olivia's downright character,
and decidedly this was not a matter to be
glossed over with synonyms for a spade. She

wanted to know how the circumstances of the
birth affected the value of the man — and so
forth. Mr. Sellwood replied as a man of the
world, and detested his replies. But the worst
was his guilty knowledge of Jack's flight. This
made him detest himself; it made him lie; and
it filled him with a relief greater than his surprise when voices came out of the darkness of
the drive, and one of them was Jack's.

Olivia ran forward.

"At last! Oh, Jack, where *have* you been?"

Mr. Sellwood never heard the answer; he was
bristling at the touch of Dalrymple, who had led
him aside.

"Entirely my doing," explained the squatter;
"but I can justify it. I mean to do so at once.
Am I right in understanding the bar sinister to
be your only objection to our friend?"

"You may put it so," said Mr. Sellwood
shortly.

"Then I shall have the pleasure of removing
the objection: the bar doesn't exist."

"Your grounds for thinking so, Mr. Dalrymple?"

"I don't think. I know. And I'm here to
prove what I know. Good heavens, do you
suppose he was no more to me than one of my
ordinary station hands? He was the son — at

all events, the stepson — of one of my oldest friends."

"The stepson! May I ask the name of your friend?"

"It is unnecessary. You have guessed it. I have a good deal to explain. Where can we go? I should like Lafont and Cripps to hear what I've got to say. Cripps especially — he will be able to check half my facts."

"I think we ought all to hear them," remarked Sellwood; "we are all interested and concerned."

"You mean the ladies? I would rather not; you can tell them afterwards; and as to the young lady, you may make your mind easy about her. If that was the only obstacle, I undertake to remove it. You can afford to trust her out of your sight."

"I shall mind my own business," snapped the Home Secretary; nevertheless, he led the way indoors with no more than a glance towards Olivia and her lover, who were still within hail; and five minutes later, as many gentlemen were empanelled in the billiard-room. Claude and Cripps and Mr. Sellwood occupied the couches at one end; Francis Freke palpitated in a corner; and Dalrymple leant against the table, his legs crossed, his arms folded, a quiet smile upon his face. He was waiting for a clock over the chimney-piece to finish striking; the hour was eleven.

"Well, gentlemen," he began, "I shall not detain you many minutes. I have certain statements to make, and any proofs that you may want I shall be happy to supply to-morrow or any time you like. Those statements will ignore, as far as possible, my own relations with the notorious Lord Maske. These I shall explain later, and you will then understand why I have hitherto held my peace concerning them. I have known all along that our friend outside — shall we call him John Dillamore? — was not and never could be the Duke of St. Osmund's; and though Mr. Cripps may look as black as his boots, he never consulted my opinion when he took John Dillamore away from my station, and it was no business of mine to interfere. Mr. Cripps seemed sufficiently positive about the matter; and, knowing what I know, I really don't blame Mr. Cripps. But this by the way. I shall first confine myself to those incidents in the Marquis's career, of which, occurring as they did at the antipodes, and as long ago as the fifties, very little has hitherto been known here in England. And I repeat that I shall afterwards be prepared to prove every word I am about to say.

"The Marquis of Maske landed in Melbourne in the early part of 1854. There for a time he cut a great dash, spent an enormous quantity of money, and indeed reached the end of his resources by the middle of the year. He then tried his luck on the Ballarat gold-fields, but his luck was out. At the diggings he sailed under an alias, and under an alias he drifted to Tasmania as early as July, 1854. And at Hobart Town, as it was then called, he met the lady for whose sake he broke, though unwittingly, one of the criminal laws of his native land.

"Now, I happen to know a good deal about that lady; but the more impersonally one enters into details of this kind the more chance has one of making such details perfectly clear to you. As it is you will find some little complications here and there. But I shall do my best to present them as intelligibly as possible; and where I fail, you will perhaps make a note of the point, and call my attention to it presently. The lady's name was Greenfield. Mrs. Greenfield was a young widow with one male child; but not, as you might suppose, a young widow with money. And the Marquis married her at Hobart under peculiar, and really rather extenuating circum-stances.

"Of course, he had a wife all the time. You

know all about that. It has leaked out through another channel — a channel I happen to have spent the last few hours in exploring. I have only just returned from the Lower Farm. I find the first wife died in 1860. But you may take my word for one thing: her husband had reason to believe she was already dead when he married for the second time in 1854.

" As a matter of fact, Eliza Hunt, as she was called, was actually at death's door in June of the latter year. On a day of which she was not expected to see the close, the late Duke wrote to his son (I happen to possess the letter, Mr. Cripps), telling him, with perhaps a pardonable satisfaction, that the end was only a question of hours; and making certain overtures which I fear only excited Lord Maske's contempt and disdain. The Marquis did not profess to be a pious man; his father did. They had parted in anger, and in anger Maske tore up his father's letter; but I collected the fragments, and preserved them — and I shall justify *that* before I'm done. Maske tore the letter to little bits. But that very week he married again on the strength of it. And I needn't tell you there was trouble when the next mail came in ! The woman was still alive; though still hopelessly — or rather hopefully — ill.

"So the couple in Tasmania lay low until their child was born — an event which proved fatal to the mother, and brought the Marquis up with a round turn, as the saying is. He was, as you may have heard, a very heartless man ; but I happen to know that he was reasonably fond of his second wife, and reasonably grieved at her death. As a matter of fact, it drove him almost crazy at the time, and embittered him for the rest of his days. The point is, however, that he was thus left with two boys — a new-born weakling and an absolutely hardy child of two, the issue of its mother's first — and only legal — marriage. The weakling he registered as he would have done had the marriage been really valid ; and, mark you, for all he knew it might be valid still. After that second letter, saying that the English wife was still hopelessly ill, he never heard again, either as to her recovery or her death, until the latter occurred some few years later. But it might have occurred while the second letter was still on the sea, for it was only a month behind the first, and they took two or three months coming in those days. And this is a point worth noting," said Dalrymple, uncrossing his arms, and for the first time making a gesture.

"It is a nice point," conceded Mr. Sellwood.

"In a nasty story!" cried the squatter, with his sardonic laugh. "No, not quite that; it's too strong a word. Still I am not here to white-wash the Marquis of Maske; indeed, the next feature of the case is wholly indefensible. You must know that all this time the exile nourished the most venomous feelings towards his family in general and the old Duke in particular. Un-lovely as they were, however, I still think there was some excuse for such sentiments; the boy had been harshly treated; he was literally forced to desert his first wife; had they lived together, in England or elsewhere, not a penny-piece would have been theirs until the death of the Duke. Hence the silence of the Hunts — for the consideration you wot of. It wasn't the sort of arrangement that would have gone on very long had the woman lived, or left a child; but she died childless, as you know; and the Hunts' subsequent policy was obvious even to the Hunts. Nor was it an arrangement calculated to increase a young man's respect for his father; in the case of Maske it intensified contempt, and created the craving for revenge. I have heard him speak so often of that revenge! He would spring an Australian heir upon the family; that was his first, and, as you know, his very last idea. He even spoke of it, as I understand, in the letter that was pinned to the tree under which he was found dead in the bush! You see it was his dominant idea in life. But the heir he spoke of was not his son at all. And that's the indefensible feature of which I spoke."

"If not his son, who was he, pray?" asked Cripps, with indignant incredulity; for his own repute was in question here.

The squatter smiled. "Can you ask? The elder of the two boys; the son of Mrs. Greenfield by her first marriage," he quietly replied.

"And what of his own son?"

"Dead."

"You will find that difficult to prove!" cried the lawyer hotly.

"Yes? I think not; he died in Sydney, where the father migrated after the mother's death; he was dead within six months of his birth. You saw the certificate of the birth in Hobart, I believe?"

"Certainly I did."

"Then here is that of the death; better keep it; you will have more use for it than I."

And the squatter turned round, and rolled the red ball up and down the board, with his quiet sinister smile, while the men on the lounges examined the document he had put in the solicitor's hands.

"It looks all right," said Cripps at length, in

a tone that made Dalrymple laugh heartily as he faced about.

"It looks all right, eh? *That's* all right! Mr. Cripps, your discernment — but excuse me! We are not here to bark and bite; we are here to clear up a mystery, at least I am. Is there any other point, gentlemen, which I can elucidate before we go any further?"

"I think there is one," said Claude, speaking nervously. "I have seen the last letter my uncle wrote, in which he mentioned an heir. I presume, in order to carry out the revenge you speak of, he called the living child by the dead child's name ——"

"Exactly. He did it deliberately. I was coming to that."

"But he seemed uncertain as to the living child's whereabouts. My point is this: where was the so-called heir at the time that last letter was written?"

"Lost," said Dalrymple, shutting his ugly lips as you shut a window. "Lost in the bush, like Maske himself, only the child's body was not found. The father had tattooed one of the eagles of his crest upon the little chap's chest — I am afraid, to further his deception. I was in all his secrets, as you see; indeed, you may call me his accomplice without offending me;

and I'm bound to say I considered the tattooing a smart idea. However, a judgment was at hand. The child was lost for many years. And the rest is easily told; it refers to *me*."

The squatter looked at Mr. Sellwood — not for the first time. As on the other occasions, however, he ran his eyes against an absolutely impassive, pink countenance.

" Mr. Sellwood may remember my little anecdote of the iron store, the Queensland blacks, and the French eagle on the chest of the stray shearer who saved all our lives ? "

Mr. Sellwood very slightly inclined his head.

" Well, that was the finding of the *soi-disant* Jack Dillamore. I knew all about him. For his father's sake, I never lost sight of him again ; for his father's sake (and also because the idea appealed to me personally) I allowed my old chum's very reprehensible plan to come off, and our friend Mr. Cripps to lay hold of my Happy Jack for the live Duke of St. Osmund's : and for the sake of some fun for my pains, I came home myself to see how matters were progressing. I'm bound to say I was disappointed. Happy Jack had grown tamer than I could have believed possible in the time. And hang me if the fellow wasn't in love ! My disgust was such that I was on the point of taking myself

off this very afternoon, and leaving the sup-
positititious Duke (whom it wasn't *my* business
to depose) to marry and save the Upper House
by the example of high morality he seemed certain to set; but at the last moment I discovered
his trouble. He was found out without my
assistance; he was cutting a worse figure than
was in any way necessary; and was about to
lose, not only the title and emoluments he had
enjoyed for some months, but the charming girl
whom he had fairly won in love. That seemed
a trifle too hard! I determined to speak out.
I have done so: and I am prepared to prove
every word I have said. The certificate now in
your pocket, Mr. Cripps, was not the only one
I had in mine. At the moment, however, there's
no more to be said — except a few words with
reference to Jack Greenfield's future. He has
suffered enough. I have been, if not at the
bottom of it, at all events to blame in the
matter. I have a little inadequate scheme of
reparation, which I shall submit to you, gentlemen, in order that you may use your influence
with Jack, if necessary. The point is that I am
never going back to Australia any more. I was
born and brought up in the old country, and
I've got the taste for it again during the few
days I've been home. Indeed, I had never lost

the taste; but I don't intend to run the risk any more. I am lucky enough to own one of the crack sheep-stations of New South Wales. I shall want a permanent manager in my absence. I needn't tell you who is the very man for *that* billet. Jack Greenfield — if he'll take it."

"A good house?" said Mr. Sellwood casually.

"The best homestead in the Riverina. Trust me for that."

Mr. Sellwood said no more. His mind was made up: better lose his daughter than have her break her heart. He could not forget the earlier experiences of the evening. The surprises of this hour were enchanting compared with the embarrassments of the last. Then he had no reason to doubt Dalrymple's word as to Jack's actual antecedents; where he doubted it, was in another matter altogether. At this point in his reflections, however, and with the inevitable discussion of the immaterial points still raging around him, Mr. Sellwood was brought to his feet by the violent opening of the billiard-room door and an agitated apparition of his wife upon the threshold. Something was the matter: had the lovers eloped? No; with Mary Freke they were at the heels of Lady Caroline, who came the length of the room at something ludicrously like a run — her very fringe awry,

and a horrified glance shooting from the corner
of each eye at the nonchalant, well-preserved
figure of Dalrymple the squatter.

"Do you know what they are saying downstairs?" cried her Ladyship, looking as far as
was possible at everybody at once. "Matthew
Hunt is here, and do you know what *he* is saying?
That neither Jack nor Claude is the Duke of St.
Osmund's, but you — you — you!" And she
turned like a podgy tigress upon none other
than the squatter himself.

"I could have told him that," remarked Mr.
Sellwood calmly; he had arrived at the con-
clusion exactly ten seconds before.

"I shall tell him something he doesn't bargain
for — the born idiot!" added the squatter *sotto
voce.*

"Then you believe it?" cried Lady Caroline
to her husband. "You must be mad!"

"Your Ladyship is so right; it would indeed
be madness to dream of entertaining so pre-
posterous a notion!" cried Mr. Cripps, who was
literally dancing with disbelief. "Even Mr.
Dalrymple will hardly go as far as that. He
has gone farther already than the law will
follow him; we'll do him the justice to hold
him irresponsible for this absurd report! He
knows as well as we do that the Marquis of

Maske was found dead in the bush; of that we have absolute proof. Even if we hadn't, who has recognized him? Has he one single witness to his identity? If so, let him be called!"

"The gentleman is excited," remarked Dalrymple, ringing the bell. "Does it really not occur to him that I might have *found myself* dead in the bush, and authenticated my own death by very obvious methods? Is it inconceivable that a young man with my then reputation should jump at the chance of dying on paper — if you will permit the expression? Such a death offers unusual advantages, a second birth among others. However, I never meant to be born again, least of all in this rather melodramatic manner; but I couldn't resist coming home to see the fun, and it serves me right to have to stop and pay the score. Witnesses? I had certainly no intention of calling any to-night; but now that my hand has been forced it can't be helped. The elder Hunt is one; knew me at sight; and here comes Stebbings for another. Shut the door behind you, Stebbings, and answer a couple of questions. It's generally supposed that you were drunk yesterday when I arrived. Were you, or were you not?"

"I was not, your Grace."

"'Your Grace,' you see!" repeated the squat-

ter. "I'm afraid that was premature, Stebbings! However, if you were not drunk, and
you certainly conveyed that impression, what
was the matter with you?"

"Nervousness!" cried Stebbings, who was
sufficiently nervous now. "I had seen the
dead! I had recognised your Grace!"

"Exactly; and I swore at you as a blind, to
explain the complete state of collapse that you
were in. That's all, Stebbings; you may go.
Jack, I see your face! You wonder you didn't
spot it at the time? Stebbings backed me up,
or else you would have done; for my part, I
confess I was more frightened when you found
us talking together in my room, when I was
packing. I assure you all, I meant to clear out
then; believe it or not, it's the case. In spite
of what I said just now, I'm not so wedded to
an English life as I fancied Jack was; and I
had no idea at the time that his position was at
all insecure. Yes, my boy, you were welcome
to the whole thing! I was going back to the
bush —— "

"*You* were going back!" cried Jack, coming
forward; and Olivia came also, flushed with a
joy that rendered her uniquely indifferent to
the great disclosure. Jack was hers. What
did it matter who was the Duke?

“To be sure I was,” said the squatter; “but now I think it will have to be you after all. What do you say to managing Carara? What do you say, Miss Sellwood, to helping him to try? You must talk to your father about it. And for heaven’s sake, Jack, don’t thank *me;* I’ve been the worst friend you ever had in your life.”

Mr. Sellwood was already speaking to his wife. Jack and their daughter stood hand-in-hand beside them. The new Duke turned his back and joined Claude on his lounge. The solicitor had beaten a retreat; the Frekes had done so before him; and the rest of their party, including Jack, did so now. But Jack returned before either Claude or the squatter had left the room.

“The worst friend I ever had!” said he reproachfully, as he took his old master’s hand. “What should I be doing to-night if it hadn’t been for you? You may say what you like; you’ve helped to make me the happiest man in all the world. I can marry her after all! Mr. Sellwood’s as white a man as I know; even Lady Caroline has just given us best! But you”—and he laid an affectionate rough hand on Claude’s shoulder—“dear old boy, what can I say to you? I’m ashamed to look you in the face. You’ve lost everything!”

Claude was very pale; the other's honest eyes were shining with sympathy beneath their bushy brows; but the new Duke laughed aloud.

"Lost everything?" he cried. "Not a bit of it! I'm not going to live for ever, and Claude's exactly where he was — the next man in. You think not? And have you known me all these years, and do you really and truly expect me to marry again? Jack — my boy — have I to tell you how it is with me? I have been a bad old lot in my time; but one woman I once loved well enough to spoil me for ever for all the rest."

He paused an instant, and it was quite a tender hand he laid on Jack's shoulder.

"And there's one man I love for her sake!"